"Phillips has done what every writer wants to do. He has brought his characters to life, and that makes this author someone to watch."

—Brandt Dodson,
author of the *Colton Parker Mystery Series*

"With powerful characters and an uncanny attention to detail, Thomas Phillips weaves a story that grabs the reader and won't let go. *The Molech Prophecy* is a book you don't want to miss."

—Joe Hilley,
author of *Sober Justice*, *Double Take*,
Electric Beach, *Night Rain*, and *The Deposition*

"*The Molech Prophecy* is a gripping, heart-pounding read with an incredible plot. Thomas Phillips is a fresh and captivating new voice in Christian fiction."

—Mark Mynheir,
homicide detective and author of *The Void*

"A fast-moving and provocative thriller. I enjoyed *The Molech Prophecy* and look forward to more from Thomas Phillips."

—James Scott Bell,
best-selling author of *Try Dying* and *The Whole Truth*

the molEch Prophecy

Thomas PHILLIPS

WHITAKER
HOUSE

Publisher's note:
This novel is a work of fiction. References to real events, organizations,
or places are used in a fictional context. Any resemblance to actual
persons, living or dead, is entirely coincidental.

THE MOLECH PROPHECY

ISBN-13: 978-1-60374-055-5 • ISBN-10: 1-60374-055-4
Printed in the United States of America
© 2008 by Thomas Phillips

Whitaker House
1030 Hunt Valley Circle
New Kensington, PA 15068
www.whitakerhouse.com

Library of Congress Cataloging-in-Publication Data

Phillips, Thomas, 1970–
The Molech prophecy / Thomas Phillips.
p.   cm.
Summary: "While investigating the events surrounding the
disappearance of his church secretary, former gang member and
new Christian Tommy Cucinelle uncovers a Wiccan plot to fulfill a
prophecy about child sacrifice to the god Molech"
—Provided by publisher.
ISBN 978-1-60374-055-5 (trade pbk.)
1. Missing persons—Fiction. 2. Wiccans—Fiction. I. Title.
PS3616.H478M65 2008
813'.6—dc22
                                                    2008008493

1 2 3 4 5 6 7 8 9 10 ᵾᴍ 14 13 12 11 10 09 08

SPECIAL THANKS

I'd like to thank my oldest son, Phil; Nancy Wheat; Julie Reitz; Greg Palmer; Christine Wrzos-Lucacci; Corrine Chorney; Darrin Frison; and Joanne Brokaw for reading through endless drafts of this manuscript and for providing valuable and honest feedback. I want to thank my wonderful agent (and talented author), Janet Benrey, not only for believing in me and my work, but also for enduring my endless e-mails. I also want to thank Christine Whitaker, Robert Whitaker, Jr., Joy Ike, Tom Cox, and Jonathan Tennent from Whitaker House. They have been supportive, inspirational and amazing to work with. I'll never forget while working on edits and rewrites, Tom told me to just "hunker down…and git-r-done." When there's a job to do, those are words to live by, I suppose.

I'd also like to give special thanks to Jars of Clay, Todd Agnew, Third Day, Casting Crowns, Kutless, and Chris Tomlin, as well as to one of my best friends, the talented Jeff Parshall. I listened endlessly to their worship CDs while writing this novel. Their impacting lyrics, unique sounds, and songs provided continual inspiration and motivation.

And last, but of course not least, I need to thank God. I'm not sure what He has in store for me, but I am anxious to see how the rest of my life plays out.

DEDICATION

This book is dedicated to my family. There is no way around it; life is full of unexpected ups and downs. Thankfully, God gave us each other so we don't have to ride those crazy rapids alone.

CHAPTER ONE

The first things I noticed when I pulled into the church parking lot were the two police cars. Instinct wanted to kick in, but I stopped myself from turning my car around. The police weren't there for me—couldn't be there for me. I'd done nothing wrong. I wasn't the same man. My days of running from the police had ended when I became a Christian. I reminded myself of this simple fact and felt a grin play across my lips. Thankfully, my days of running from the police ended four years ago.

On any given Sunday, I have come to expect many things from Faith Community Church. And why not? I have been attending weekly services for years. I expect smiles from Faith's Greet Team— from those helping direct cars in the parking lot to those handing out programs and pencils at the sanctuary doors. I expect powerful worship music, a variety of jokes from Pastor Ross—some funny, some not so funny—and I expect, each week, a message that will impact the way I live the rest of my life.

But what I did not expect this morning was what I saw next: the complete defacing of the church building. Black spray paint covered the pecan-colored bricks in horrific graffiti.

After parking, I sat silently in the car, taking it all in. A large pentagram—an encircled, upside-down, five-pointed star—was displayed at the center of it all. Painted on every other available surface were words like "Death," "Die," "Faggots," "Hypocrites," and "God Is Dead."

Seeing all of the graffiti felt like a punch to the gut. Faith Community was like my second home; the people who attended were like my second family. It was impossible *not* to take this attack personally.

Slowly, I climbed out of the car, ignoring the early November morning chill. The wind blew relentlessly all around me, howling and moaning as if it too was furious and saddened and confused by the desecration.

Other cars pulled into the lot. The people getting out of them emerged as slowly as I must have. I could see the stunned expressions on their faces— dropped jaws and wide eyes that surely matched my own.

Who would vandalize a church like this? I wondered

as I walked toward the entrance. As I stopped in front of the pentagram and took in the mess that attempted to dirty my church, I realized that whoever did this was hurting—hurting badly. That thought did not stifle the anger—the righteous anger—I felt boiling deep inside.

I nodded a grim good morning to the greeter who held the front door open as I walked into the church. The atrium is usually packed with people mingling before the start of the service. Free coffee, hot cocoa, and doughnuts set out on a table each and every week encourage people to arrive early for fellowship.

This morning, however, only a few people lingered in the atrium. Whispers were all I heard. As I entered the sanctuary I saw that this was where everyone had gathered. I usually sit toward the back, far right, as if there were assigned seating. The things I'd seen outside left me feeling hollow and alone. Today, I sat closer to the front, middle row.

I nodded hello to people here and there. Many sat with heads bowed, deep in prayer. I decided praying would be a good use of the extra time before the service.

I tried to cope with a flood of mixed emotions, such as anger, sadness, confusion, disbelief, and then, once again, anger. Instead of praying, questions ended up filling my mind: *Who could do such a thing? Why would someone do such a thing? How are we going to get that filth off the bricks? If I ever get my....* I broke off the last thought before it got out of hand. *I'm in a church,* I reminded myself. *There is no place for thoughts like that, but especially not in a church.*

The service did not start the way services normally did. The church band usually opened worship with a fast-tempo song, one that got those present up on their feet, clapping and singing along, and one that brought those lingering in the atrium into the sanctuary.

Today, in dead silence, Senior Pastor Ross Lobene walked out and stood center stage, gripping the podium. He seemed at a loss for words. I think he knew what he wanted to say but was afraid that if he tried speaking too soon, he might lose his composure. I wouldn't blame him.

As usual, roughly two thousand people filled most of the available seats. Two large projection screens hung on the wall at either side of the stage. Both showed a close-up of the pastor's face. He could not hide his red eyes—or stop his quivering lips.

Pastor Ross opened a Bible, and when he finally started to speak, his voice was weak and shaky, as if he were on the verge of crying. "I want to read

Thomas Phillips

Matthew, chapter five, verses ten through twelve: *'God blesses those who are persecuted for doing right, for the Kingdom of heaven is theirs. God blesses you when people mock you and persecute you and lie about you and say all sorts of evil things against you because you are my followers. Be happy about it! Be very glad! For a great reward awaits you in heaven. And remember, the ancient prophets were persecuted in the same way.'*

He bowed his head.

I felt sorrowful pain in my chest.

"Shock. Pure shock," Pastor Ross said. "You don't think stuff like *this* will happen *here*. It will happen elsewhere, like in run-down, gang-ridden areas, so we think. But from what I know of human nature, it happens everywhere, because people can be dark-hearted everywhere. God is always in control, and He wants us to learn to deal with problems in God-honoring ways. I have come to realize through this incident, and through other incidents that have occurred in our church family, that our enemy, Satan, attacks those churches that are a threat to him and his evil ways."

I nodded in agreement, listening intently and watching as Pastor Ross released his white-knuckled grip on the podium and began to come into his own. He paced back and forth on the stage, addressing the congregation, righteous fire heating this impromptu sermon.

The mol̶E̶c̶h̶ Prophecy

"Jesus tells us in Revelation three, verses fourteen through seventeen, that He will spit out of His mouth the church whose people are lukewarm in their faith, because they are neither hot nor cold. It is my desire for Faith Community Church to be a church that is hot, making a difference for Christ and His kingdom in Rochester and the surrounding area."

As Pastor Ross paused, he stroked the sandy-colored goatee that covered his chin and used a handkerchief to wipe away the beads of sweat that formed on his bald head. "This, friends, this is a great opportunity for us to love our enemies as ourselves." He pointed out at us and then pointed back at himself. "It is my desire to see everyone at Faith truly model this command from Christ and not become bitter by this incident. I pray that we have an opportunity to minister to the needs of the person or people responsible, so we can share the life-changing message of the gospel with them.

"I have known many people who have been enslaved in the bondage of satanism and witchcraft, and although the hold these things have on them is strong, it is no match for our all-powerful, all-loving God. It will take time, but if we can be models of Christ's love to this person, I have full confidence that he will become a child of the light instead of a slave to the darkness." A second, brief pause followed. Then Pastor Ross added, "Don't get me wrong. I also hope that the person who did this crime is caught and processed fairly through our justice system."

I tried to let my own anger subside. If Pastor Ross could move on, so could I. All I needed now was help unclenching my hands, which had been rolled into solid fists since the beginning of service.

CHAPTER TWO

Pastor Ross stood by the doors as people filed out of the church, shaking hands with some, hugging others, and sharing words about this and that.

I rarely stood in line. The first few times I visited the church, I had—there was no obligation, but I always felt funny going around the line and bolting out the door. Pastor Ross always seemed to call out a good-bye to me, even if he was in the middle of a conversation with someone who had waited in line.

Today was no different. I tried getting out without his seeing me.

"Hey, Tommy," he said.

"Great message," I said. I meant it.

"Look, can you hang out a bit? I need to talk with you." He stared at me, completely ignoring the woman standing in front of him.

What could he need to talk to me about?

"Just for a few minutes," he pleaded.

"Oh, yeah. No problem," I said. I stood there.

"Want to go wait for me in my office? I'll be right in."

I shrugged and nodded. "Sure."

He was five six, five seven tops, whereas I was five-ten. He was a slim 160 pounds, while I spent most of my free time at the gym tipping the scales at a solid 180. Close to fifty, Pastor Ross was bald except for his blondish goatee. But he wore his baldness well, probably because he didn't try hiding it. At twenty-six, I had a full head of shoulder length black hair that I brushed back and tied in a ponytail.

I greeted a few people as I made my way back toward Pastor Ross's office. The congregation of people, for the most part, was headed for the parking lot. Few lingered. One guy began collecting trash. Another removed a broom from a closet by the restrooms.

The secretary was not around. Behind the desk where she usually sat was Pastor Ross's door. It was open. I tentatively walked around the secretary's desk and poked my head into the office. I knew the pastor was still at the front of the church, and though he'd told me to wait in his office, just walking in made me a bit uncomfortable.

I'd never been in Pastor Ross's office before. It was brighter than I expected. Windows with open blinds allowed natural light to fill the room. Several framed black-and-white photographs of the pastor and his family decorated the white walls. A closed laptop, gold nameplate, office phone, and calendar were all that adorned the desk. The only visible clutter came from packed-full bookcases that lined one entire wall.

"Tommy, thank you for hanging back."

Startled, I turned to see Pastor Ross standing behind me. He opened his arms, and we hugged quickly.

"Please, come in. Have a seat." I sat in the chair across from his desk. He closed the door gently before sitting on the edge of the desk. "How's everything been going?"

Small talk. "Fine," I said. The hairs on the back of my neck tingled. Obviously, the pastor had a purpose for this chitchat. I couldn't help feeling like a suspect about to be interrogated by the police.

"What'd you think about that graffiti?" he asked.

My stomach muscles knotted. Did he think I was responsible? I did not expect accusations from my pastor. I was about to stand up when he got to his feet.

"It's awful," Pastor Ross said. "I'm speechless, too. The good thing is the police have some pretty solid leads." He moved to the burgundy leather chair behind his desk and sat down, leaned back, and folded his hands in his lap. "Wondering what I want to talk with you about?"

"I'm a bit curious, yes," I admitted.

"This is a little awkward for me," he said as he leaned forward and rested his elbows on the desk. "I hate bringing up your past—the *you* before you became a Christian—but I need your help."

Pastor Ross knew all about my past. I had confessed my sins, my old ways, in front of him and about twelve other men during a men's prayer meeting. I'd moved beyond my past because of Jesus. I did not want to revisit even the *memories* of my old self—unless it was something God wanted me to do.

"Nancy Callahan," he said.

"Your secretary," I said.

He nodded. "She's gone. I don't think she quit. Or she might have, I'm not sure. All I know is she's gone."

"Gone?"

"Gone. I called the police," he said.

"And?"

"They went to her apartment. The landlord said she paid a few extra bucks to get out of her lease. Couple of days later a moving truck backed up to the place. She filled it with her stuff and left. The police didn't see a problem with that."

The mo|Ech Prophecy

I didn't see a problem with it, either. "She's a grown woman."

"That's what they said, too. Leaving your job without telling the boss and moving out of your apartment are not crimes, nor do they constitute foul play." Pastor Ross stood up and turned to look out the window, his hands on his hips. "It just doesn't feel right to me."

"What doesn't?" I said to the image reflected in the window.

"The way she left. The way she'd been acting the last several weeks. Something was going on. Something was bothering her. I have no idea what, but I could feel it, you know?" He frowned. "I'm good at reading people. And with her, it was pretty obvious that something wasn't right."

I thought I was good at reading people, too. Something was definitely wrong here. "So you want me to do what? Find her?"

Pastor Ross turned and smiled at me. His entire expression softened. The worry wrinkles that had creased his brow had smoothed out. "Exactly. Find her."

"And when I find her, then what?"

"Nothing."

I shook my head, confused.

"I mean, I want you to make sure she's all right.

Maybe stay on her for a bit and make sure she's not in any kind of trouble," he explained.

"And then tell you where she is?" I asked. I had to ask. Just having a talk like this, whether Ross was a pastor or not, poked and prodded at my old life, awakening a suspicious part of me that I thought I'd left behind forever.

"No, you don't have to tell me where she is. I'm not trying to track her down."

"You're not?" I asked. I'd known guys who wanted women found—women who cleared out bank accounts before leaving town, women who ran off with their lover's best friend, boss, or brother-in-law. And I'd known exactly what would happen to those women when I told those guys where to find them. At the time, I couldn't care less about the fate of the women I tracked down. All I cared about was my fee—that it was paid in cash and on time.

"I don't need to know where she is. I'm just worried about her. I feel like I failed her. Something was bothering her, and I never really asked. I never got around to seeing if there was anything I could do to help. I feel like I let her down," he said. "I'm always so consumed with making sure this church runs efficiently and smoothly that sometimes I lose focus of what my role as a pastor really is all about. I'm not a businessman, but running this church forces me to wear a businessman's hat. I'm a pastor, a shepherd. What kind of shepherd lets his sheep wander off, alone and scared?"

"She was scared?" I asked, maybe a bit too quickly.

He just laughed and then shrugged. "What sheep isn't scared when it separates from the flock?"

Nice answer.

Someone knocked on the door. Before Pastor Ross could respond, the door opened a crack.

"Ross?" Assistant Pastor Alan Reddinger poked his head into the office.

"I'm in a meeting," Pastor Ross said.

The door opened all the way, and Pastor Alan walked in. "Oh, hey, Tommy," he said.

"Hey," I said and stood up. We shook hands.

Pastor Alan looked like he might be nineteen, with skin so smooth and white I couldn't help wondering if he'd ever had to shave a day in his life. His brown hair was wavy, and long bangs dangled down to the top of his nose. He constantly had to brush the hair from his eyes. Maybe five ten, one fifty, he was rail thin, wiry. He was single, and it was obvious that all the women here loved him.

"Sorry to interrupt. Two quick things. First, your wife's looking for you, and second, I brought by a draft of my sermon for the midweek service. Can you read through it?" Pastor Alan produced a few sheets of paper and handed them over.

"Alan, you don't need to keep reviewing your messages with me. You do a wonderful job at preparing and delivering the message at every midweek," Pastor Ross said.

Pastor Alan raised his eyebrows, begging silently.

Pastor Ross sighed in resignation. "Fine. Fine. I'll look through it. Tell Holly I'll be out in a second."

"You got it. Thanks. And if something needs to be changed, just let me know. You won't hurt my feelings. That's how I learn, through your critique. I'll edit it—"

"Alan!"

"Sorry. Okay. I didn't mean to interrupt," Pastor Alan said, waving goodbye and closing the office door as he left.

Ross smiled and shook his head as he stared for a moment at the closed door. "Please, Tommy, sit back down."

I sat, not sure what to say.

"Will you do it?" he asked.

"Just find her, make sure she's all right?"

He nodded. "That's all."

"I don't have to tell you where she is?"

"No."

The mo|Ech Prophecy

"She might not still be in Rochester, you know."

"I'm willing to pay you for your time. It can't be much."

"I'll just need expenses. I'll do it on my time. I can't let it interfere with my job," I said.

"That's not right. Let me pay you."

"Just expenses." I stood up. We shook hands. "You have a picture of her? One I can take to show around in case I need to?"

We left his office and went to her desk. He lifted a framed photo of Nancy, with raven-black hair, white-white skin, and hazel-colored eyes, snuggling closely to a calico cat. He removed it from the frame. "Will this do?"

"She leave a lot of personal stuff here?" I asked.

"Not really. Just this picture."

I took the photograph. "It should be fine. What was her address?" I asked, picking up a pen from the desk. He gave it to me. I wrote it on the back of the photo and tucked it into my coat pocket. "I guess I'll get started."

Chapter Three

Nancy Callahan lived in the town of Greece, which bordered the city of Rochester and Lake Ontario, the smallest of the Great Lakes. Unfortunately, the highly-polluted Genesee River spilled into the lake. In the summer, the water's stench wafted throughout the area.

Nancy's apartment complex, Oak Tree Meadows, was located just off the parkway, a couple miles south of Charlotte Beach. I knew people who used to live there. The cheap rent is what sold them on the place, but once they realized how often the cops came around to handle domestic disputes, drug busts, burglaries, and robberies, they quickly moved on.

The complex was set up more or less in the shape of a horseshoe. An Oak Tree Meadows sign had been placed at the entrance, forming a barrier that separated traffic going in and out of the neighborhood. Oak Tree Meadows had both apartments and townhouses—apartments at the front of the place and townhouses in back.

The mo|Ech Prophecy

At the center of it all was the front office and clubhouse, complete with a workout and multipurpose room. Behind the clubhouse were an in-ground swimming pool, four tennis courts, and one of those huge plastic playgrounds surrounded by cedar wood chips. As I drove past the front office I noticed that the pool had been covered for winter, and that a woman was sitting on a bench reading a paperback novel while three little kids ran wild on the playground. She watched me over her book as I drove past slowly and continued around the complex.

Nancy lived in townhouse 2112, which was next to 2114. I parked in a spot a few spaces down and sat in the car for a moment, taking in the things around me. Amid all the cars parked on the opposite side of Nancy's townhouse, one was backed into a spot and running. Exhaust fumes puffed out of the tailpipe. From where I sat, I couldn't tell if anyone sat behind the wheel.

The fact that Nancy's townhouse didn't have curtains on any of the windows made the place look vacant.

For a late Sunday morning, the complex seemed extremely quiet. Except for the lady at the playground and the kids she was with, I didn't see anyone. I opened my car door and immediately noticed the drop in temperature as the warmth inside was replaced with icy air. Climbing out of my car, I tensed the muscles in my arms and hands to keep from shivering. I stuffed my hands into the pockets of my leather coat, walked up the sidewalk, and climbed the front steps.

Peeking in the nearest window, I saw no furniture. I couldn't see anything hanging on any of the walls. The place was cleaned out, that much was clear.

I knew that going through someone's mailbox was a federal crime, but Pastor Ross had assured me that Nancy had moved out of her place. So was it still breaking the law if no one officially lived here? I wondered about that as I opened her old mailbox.

Bingo! I removed mail and walked back to my car. I climbed in and backed out of the parking spot. I wanted to look through the mail, but not until I was clear of the place, or before I'd spoken to someone in the front office.

I knocked on the front office door and pushed it open in one motion. A buzzer sounded, signaling my arrival. Faux dark wood paneling and rubber plants made up the atmosphere of the place. To the right sat a young woman, early twenties, blond hair, dark eyes. She wore a cream-colored blouse under a black blazer. Her red painted nails were poised over a computer keyboard.

"Can I help you?" she asked.

I moved closer to her desk, slowly though. I might be a mellow Christian now, but my overall appearance still screamed *dangerous thug*. "I was hoping to visit my cousin, Nancy," I said. "She lives in one of your townhouses. Only, when I got there, it looked like she'd left, like she moved out or something."

"Does your cousin Nancy have a last name?"

"Callahan," I said. "She was in twenty-one twelve."

The woman's eyes widened. Not a lot, but enough to show that she knew whom I was talking about, a hint of recognition. Still, she let her fingers tap away at the keyboard. "Twenty-one twelve is vacant," she said.

"Well, I just told you that," I said. I let out a polite laugh, like oh-golly-gee. "That's why I came to see you. I'm trying to figure out where my cousin went."

"I'm not allowed to give out information on current or former tenants," she said.

I looked for a nameplate on the lady's desk and found it. "Sally, Nancy ain't a current or former tenant. She's my cousin."

"Regardless, I can't give you any information. All I can tell you for sure is that unit twenty-one twelve is vacant and will be ready to lease Monday of next week."

"So how long has it been vacant?" I asked, deciding to lean a shoulder against the wall, taking on a completely nonthreatening stance.

"I can't tell you that."

I smiled, my continued attempt at being charming. "I don't want to cause you no trouble. Nancy, see, she's had a falling out with the whole family. I think she's mad at all of us. I can't stand it, you know, having her mad at me. All I want to do is tell her I'm sorry."

Sally softened. I saw it in her eyes, the way she slowly blinked, as if batting those eyelids at me. "I can't tell you when she moved out. But," she said, "what I can tell you is that it takes two weeks to get a townhouse ready for new tenants." Sally leaned back in her chair, her fingers tapping the wrist rest along the bottom of her keyboard.

"And the place will be ready to rent next Monday. So maybe she's been gone a week?" I said, not really asking.

"Maybe a week."

I nodded my thanks and stood up straight. "I appreciate it. It's not good for family to fight."

I reached for the doorknob, and then I stopped.

Sally had not gone back to work. She'd been watching me. "If I wanted to send her a letter...."

"I would not be able to give you information like that, cousin or not—and I strongly suspect it's 'not.'" She eyed me suspiciously, like she thought maybe I was more than likely one of Nancy's ex-boyfriends or something. "But I will tell you she did not leave any forwarding address information with us."

"Fair enough. Thanks."

I decided I'd head home, but on the drive back toward my apartment, I couldn't help noticing the dark blue car behind me. I did not see it pull out of Nancy's complex when I did, but I clearly recognized it as the car that had been sitting idle in the parking lot while I checked Nancy's mailbox. Since leaving Oak Tree Meadows and getting on the main road, it had remained consistently three car lengths behind.

I was anxious to check the mail but did not want to lead anyone back to where I lived.

Then I laughed out loud.

I was looking for a missing church secretary. I was tracking down a woman who decided to up and quit her job and move out of her townhouse. What was wrong with me? This wasn't dangerous. No one was following me. Why in the world would someone be following me? Sure, that may be the dark blue car I'd seen at Oak Tree Meadows, but it could be headed anywhere in the city—coincidently going in the same direction as I.

To prove how crazy-paranoid I was acting, I pulled over to the side of the road and let traffic pulse on by.

I watched as the dark blue car passed. I could only see one person in the car, but not what that person looked like. No one was following....

The dark blue car made a left into the corner gas station lot at the next light.

It did not make sense that I'd been followed. What made sense was that the driver of the dark blue car from the apartment complex where Nancy had lived needed gas. I pulled back into the flow of traffic, stayed in the far right lane, and drove past the gas station.

I could see the dark blue car parked beside a gas pump. Obviously, the driver needed gas. And I was losing my cool. It was expected. This wasn't how I made my living, not anymore. Cloak and dagger stuff just wasn't me.

Getting ready to change lanes, I glanced into my rearview mirror. The dark blue car was pulling out of the gas station and was falling in line behind me, three car lengths back.

Even I realized there was no way the driver had bought gas that quickly. Only seconds had lapsed since I'd seen him. I knew one thing for sure: professionals weren't following me. Professionals tail people using a two- or three-car tag system so that the mark *doesn't* get suspicious.

No, whoever was following me was strictly an amateur. Two questions nagged at me. *Who was following me?* And, *Why in the world would someone be following me?*

Chapter Four

Knowing I had a tail, I postponed heading home. No reason to lead anyone to my apartment. It was almost noon. I was hungry. I needed a place where I could sit and look through Nancy's mail.

Off Long Pond Road was a sports bar called The Huddle. It sat in the corner of a small L-shaped plaza, sandwiched between a pizza place and a liquor store, and was marked by a single door under an awning. I parked and quickly rifled through Nancy's mail, taking out the only envelope that looked interesting and tucking it under my visor. The rest I shoved in my coat pocket.

The Huddle. Just seeing the tucked-away doorway almost made me feel claustrophobic. Years had passed since the last time I was here. Thankfully, looks were deceiving. Once inside I remembered just how big the place really was.

To the right were video games, pool tables, foosball tables, and dart games. Laws outlawing smoking in public places made bars more accessible to families. Kids crowded the game area, feeding the machines coin after coin.

Everywhere else, tables and booths encircled a large U-shaped bar. Giant flat-screen televisions were mounted to the wall above the tables and booths every three feet or so; six sets hung over the bar so that at least two screens were visible no matter where you sat in the joint.

The place was pretty crowded. Men and women were everywhere, eating, talking, and laughing. Music was piped in, either from a jukebox I couldn't see or from the bar's own music system. The video games from the corner beeped, buzzed, rang, and clanged. People talked and laughed in loud voices in order to be heard over all of the other sounds.

At the bar I ordered a large meatball and mozzarella sub with French fries and a Coke. The barmaid, a pretty brunette, smiled absently and handed me a placard tent with the number thirteen on it. I found an empty booth near the back and sat facing the front door. I displayed my number thirteen at the edge of the table so that when my food was ready the waitress would have no trouble finding me.

The Buffalo Bills pregame show was on most of the television sets. Normally, this would bother me. Even though I only live sixty miles east of Buffalo, I'm not a Bills fan. Today, the Bills were playing my team: the Miami Dolphins. It was a division game, and it was a big one because the two were battling to see who would drop into last place. I wish I were being sarcastic. Both teams looked terrible so far this year. Though my loyalty to the Dolphins would never waiver, I'd already written off this season and was looking forward to a first-round draft pick next year.

As the front door opened and a woman entered the bar, I realized that she appeared vaguely familiar. I watched as she looked around tentatively. Perhaps her husband or boyfriend was meeting her here. She seemed out of place, uncomfortable, as she clutched her purse close to her chest and attempted to see the face of every person in the place.

I recognized her from somewhere—an old girlfriend? I didn't think so. I'd like to think I'd remember a woman as pretty as this. Her red hair, fair skin, and green eyes were a captivating collection.

Though I didn't mean to stare, when our eyes met, she did her best not to look away quickly and walked over to the bar. She knew who I was, too, but not because we'd dated, and not because we knew each other. It was just a hunch, but I thought she might be the one driving the dark blue car.

Along with Nancy's mail in the inside pocket of my leather coat was the picture Pastor Ross had given me. I pulled out the photo, looked at it, and then put it away. Despite the contrast in hair color, Nancy and the redhead had to be related.

The redhead sat on a bar stool and tried to appear as if she wasn't keeping an eye on me. I stood up and slowly made my way to the bar, my eyes never leaving her. The closer I got, the more nervous she looked. Her hands fidgeted with the straps on her purse. Her gaze darted around the room, as if searching for an escape route. I got the distinct feeling this beautiful woman thought I was going to harm her, right here, right now, in front of all these people.

When I got too close, she jumped to her feet, knocking some five-year-old kid to the ground. Though she said, "Sorry," and helped the boy back up to his feet, she kept looking from me to the door she'd entered just moments ago.

"You following me?" I asked.

Without an answer, she pushed past the kid she'd just helped up, knocking him down again, and ran full steam out of The Huddle. All eyes were on me. I raised my hands and eyebrows, making sure everyone knew I hadn't touched her.

I thought about going back to my booth, waiting for my food, and settling in to watch the football game, but I remembered my promise to Pastor Ross. He had asked me to find Nancy. Maybe the easiest way to do that would be by talking to the redhead.

Outside, I saw her by the dark blue car, fumbling around in her purse, maybe searching for car keys.

I'd already scared her half to death. And though I'll admit it was funny, it wasn't something I wanted to do a second time. "I'm not sure who you think I am," I called out.

She ignored me, but I knew she could hear me. She dropped her keys as I spoke. "You're Nancy's sister," I announced.

She looked right at me. I saw tears, but I also saw anger and fear. I knew what anger looked like, and I also knew the look of fear. Her eyes were wide, her lips quivered—they were full lips, naturally red lips. Behind those lips I saw white teeth, clenched and grinding.

"Ever hear of Faith Community Church?" I continued. "I go there. Your sister is the pastor's assistant, or was."

She'd picked up the keys and unlocked her door. Her hand rested on the handle, but it didn't seem like she was in the same hurry to run away. There was plenty of distance between us. Maybe she thought there was enough distance that if I ran at her, she could climb into the car before I reached her. I'm not sure that would be true, but if it made her feel more comfortable, then fine.

"Pastor Ross, your sister's boss, asked me if I could help him find her. She stopped coming to work, and it looks like she up and moved. Pastor Ross wants to make sure she's all right," I said. My food had to be almost ready. As pretty as this woman was, I didn't want my sub to get cold, I didn't want to lose my booth, and I didn't want to miss kickoff. "I'm guessing you don't know where she is either or you wouldn't have been staking out her place." Redhead just stared at me. I'd given it a shot. "You take it easy," I said, turning to go back into the bar.

"I saw you take her mail," she shouted.

She speaks! "That's right," I said, facing her. "It's obvious she doesn't live there anymore. I thought it might help me figure out where she went. Do you know where she went?"

Redhead fell silent again.

"Look, I ordered some food. I can't stand the cold. I'm going back in. You want to join me? We can talk, maybe figure out what's up?" I stood there for three seconds, one, two, three, and when Redhead did not move or make a sound, I went back into the bar and followed a waitress carrying the tray of food to my booth.

I asked the waitress to bring me an extra plate and an extra Diet Coke. When they arrived, I reluctantly cut my sub in two, placing half of it on the second plate, which I pushed across the table.

As I had hoped, Redhead walked into the bar a second time. I looked straight ahead, keeping my eyes on the large-screen television mounted over a table at the opposite end of the room. Kickoff was moments away. The bad thing about watching the game here, alone, was that I couldn't hear the announcers, which was why I preferred watching games at home. And this was a bar for Bills fans. I was dining in enemy territory.

I saw her slowly making her way toward my booth. As I picked up my half of the meatball sub, I glanced at her, smiled, and nodded for her to join me. She looked around, perhaps making sure I was talking to her.

"Have a seat," I said.

"Expecting someone?"

"You," I said. "I got you a Diet Coke."

"And that is…?"

"A meatball sub. I can't eat in front of people unless they're eating, too. You can have some fries," I said and pointed to the plate of fries in the center of the table. "But I don't like ketchup, so if you want ketchup make sure you only put it on the fries you want to eat."

She stood beside the booth like a statue.

"Sit down. This ain't a date. I told you, I can't eat in front of people."

"I want my sister's mail," she demanded, refusing to sit.

I bit into my sub, turning my attention back to the game.

"I thought you couldn't eat in front of people who weren't eating," she said.

"Changed my mind. Look, sit or don't sit," I said.

"I want the mail."

There was no reason I should keep it. "Why were you sitting in your sister's apartment complex watching the place?"

"I want the mail."

"Did you know there was mail in the box? I'll bet you did. I'll bet you wanted to get it yourself but didn't want to get caught," I said. Her eyes were so green, her lips so full, so red. "Where's your sister?"

"I want the mail."

"You don't know where your sister is, but you're worried about her, aren't you?"

I waited for her to demand the mail again. If she had, I would have given it to her. She had more of a right to that mail than I did. But she didn't ask for it. I could tell she was worried. "Please, sit down."

She sat, pushing the half a meatball sub away from her. "Thank you, but no thank you."

Over Redhead's shoulder I noticed that the Bills had won the coin toss and elected to receive. The Dolphins lined up, kicked the ball, and the game was underway.

"What's your name?" I asked.

"I don't see how that's any of your business."

Lord, give me patience with this one, I silently prayed. I held out my hand. "I'm Tommy," I said. "Tommy Cucinelle."

She regarded my hand for what seemed like minutes before she finally shook it. "I'm Stacey."

"Stacey," I said. "When's the last time you saw your sister?"

CHAPTER FIVE

When she didn't respond, I asked a second time. "Stacey, when's the last time you saw your sister?"

She pursed her lips, wrinkled her nose. "Why did your pastor ask you to look for my sister?"

She wasn't going to answer my questions until she felt comfortable. It looked like the only way she'd feel comfortable was to ask me questions and see if I'd answer them. "I told you. He was worried about her. She stopped coming to work without calling in. The way I understand it, your sister wasn't like that. She was very dependable. When he tried reaching her and couldn't, he grew more concerned and even called the police to make sure she was all right."

"So are you with the police?"

I almost laughed. "Me? No."

"A private investigator?"

I sipped my Coke. I knew what she was after. "No."

"So why you? Why would the pastor of a church—a pretty huge church, from what I understand—go to someone like you for help?"

Someone like me? I let it slide.

My cell phone rang. I held up a finger. "Excuse me a sec." I looked at the phone. Tay. I answered. "Hey, buddy, what's going on?" He was at my place. Stopped by to watch the game with me.

"I'm planning to watch the game at The Huddle," I said. "I can explain, but believe me, it's getting to be a long story. You want to come down? Okay. I got a booth. See you then."

I put the phone away. "You want to know what's confusing me, if I can speak honestly here?"

"Oh, by all means, speak honestly. I would expect nothing less from a Christian," she said.

"You're not a Christian?" I asked.

"Not like my sister, not like the people at your church. You people take religion too far, to the extreme. No offense, but I think you lose touch with reality."

"No offense taken, believe me." In fact, it was a compliment. "But here's what's confusing me. I have absolutely no idea what's going on and I get an uneasy feeling that there is a lot going on."

She stared at me for a moment and then slumped back into the booth, as if letting some of her guard down, finally.

The ~~mol Ech~~ Prophecy

"All I know is what Pastor Ross told me, what I've told you. He asked me to find your sister, to make sure she's all right, and that's it," I said.

"He paying you?"

"Expenses," I said.

"Like this lunch?" she asked.

I thought about it. "Yeah. I'm on the clock. So this lunch would be an expense." She eyed the meatball sub I'd left for her. "Take it," I said.

She took it.

For the next few minutes we ate our subs. I wasn't worried about my half getting cold. I was just thankful for the time she allowed for me to actually eat it—and watch some of the game. Miami was down by seven; we were only a few minutes into the opening quarter.

As we sipped a fresh round of sodas, Stacey talked about Nancy.

"She'd been acting funny lately," she said. "Something was going on in her life that was making her miserable."

There was more. She just didn't seem ready to share. It didn't matter. I was enjoying my time with her. I could not stop looking into those eyes. "You two close?" I prodded.

"*Were* close. Not so much lately," she said. There it was again, the hint that more lurked just below the surface.

"What changed?" I asked.

"She changed. Once she got all *religious*, she just wasn't the same. We weren't the same. Nothing was."

"When was that?" I asked.

"You sure you're not a cop?" I shook my head. "A reporter, then?"

"Nothing of the sort, I assure you. You were saying the relationship changed. How long ago was that?"

"Almost ten years, but really the last five have been the toughest between us—when she started going to that church of yours," she said. "I have absolutely nothing against God. I don't. I believe in Him and everything, but everything Nancy did was 'God' this and 'thank Jesus' that. It got nauseating after awhile."

"So if something was bothering her, she wouldn't have told you?" I asked.

"I think she'd have told me. The problem was, I never asked."

She used her straw to stab at the ice cubes in her drink. She held back her emotions as best she could. I watched closely. From where I sat I could clearly sense the battle for control being waged inside her. The pain on her face was evident. Her lips puckered and pouted.

"Stacey," I said.

"No. I mean, how could I *not* ask her what was wrong? I saw something was bothering her, you know?" Whether she knew it or not, she was crying. Tears streamed down her cheeks. She made no attempt to wipe them away. "She wanted me to ask, too. I could tell. She was too stubborn to bring anything up, too proud, but she wanted me to ask."

I pulled a chunk of napkins out of the dispenser and set them in front of her. "Thank you," she said, as she dried the tears and dabbed at her nose.

"You don't have any idea what was bothering her?"

Stacey looked at me like I had two heads. "Did you even hear what I said?"

"Sorry," I said. "Do you have any idea where she might have gone?"

"You know what? There's no way you're a cop. Why would I have been sitting in her apartment complex if I knew where she might have gone?" Stacey rolled up the used napkin and kept it crinkled inside her fist.

"So when was the last time you saw her?" I asked, for a third time.

"Today's Sunday, right? So it was a week ago—on Monday."

"You saw her?"

"I was at her place. She looked so sad, nervous." She shook her head as if silently berating herself for failing her sister. Then again, maybe she had.

"Your parents?" I offered.

"I called them. They haven't heard from her."

"They live around here?"

"Hilton," she said. Two towns over. "And no, they haven't heard from her, either. They're worried, too."

I could only imagine.

"You got a friend meeting you here?"

I nodded.

She stood up. "I've got to go. Thank your pastor for lunch."

"Will do," I said.

She turned but did not walk away. "Now, can I have my sister's mail?"

I pulled the mail out of my coat pocket. "Can I get your cell number?"

She looked annoyed as she took the mail out of my hand. "I don't think so."

"In case I have questions or come across anything? Okay," I said. "Never mind."

"I'm sorry. I thought you were hitting on me."

The moĮEch Prophecy

We exchanged numbers, entering them directly into our phones.

When she left, I shook my head. I turned my attention to the game. Or rather, I watched the game. My attention was on Stacey. I had an idea of what she was going through. I thought of my little brother.

Although I'd taken Stacey's number, and despite how pretty she was, I had no intention of calling her. My job was to find Nancy. Stacey did not seem to have any helpful information. Instead, I'd have to keep looking on my own.

CHAPTER SIX

Moments after Stacey left, Ayenta "Tay" Brown walked into The Huddle. When he saw me, he smiled. I waved him over. I stood as we hugged and shook hands. He was my best friend. We'd known each other since grade school, a time when we were anything but friends. Being one of only a few white kids in a predominately black and Hispanic inner-city school, I stood out like a sore thumb. Everything was gang oriented. You either joined one or spent your days running from them.

No one wanted a skinny little white kid in his gang back then—that is, until one day in the sixth grade when Tay was getting the stuffing kicked out of him in the boys' bathroom. Three kids had Tay cowering in the fetal position in a corner by the sinks. They stomped on him with the heels of their boots, kicked him in the ribs, and even got down low so they could throw punches.

I walked in on this. I had no idea it was Tay getting beaten up; all I saw was three on one. So I rushed to his defense. Aside from giving two kids black eyes and landing a few other lucky blows, I wound up on the ground next to Tay, sharing in his relentless punishment.

Once I healed up, Tay and his gang approached me out on the school yard during recess. At first I thought I was in for another beating for having interfered in gang-related business. The eight of them all wore grim, hard expressions. Not a smile to be seen—until Tay held out his fist. He smiled and nodded approvingly. I punched my fist to his. We hugged. The others crowded around. Pats on the back were delivered, words of appreciation spoken. I was almost in the gang.

Almost.

At midnight, if I wanted in, I was to meet them in the playground at the center of the projects on Joseph Avenue. Sneaking out of my house was not a problem. My little brother, Nicholas, shared a room with me. He slept like a rock. I climbed out the window and ran to the playground.

Adrenaline bubbled inside me, pumped through my veins and arteries so fast I thought my heart would explode. I knew what was going to happen that night. Initiation. I also remember hoping no one would show.

They were all there. They stood under the monkey bars, most of them smoking. One of the kids took swigs out of a bottle wrapped in a brown paper bag. When they saw me they stood, crushed out their cigarettes in the mulch, and formed a circle around me.

If you wanted in, you had to fight them. All of them. All at once. To get the night started and over with, I charged first. Like a bull I ran at one guy in particular. And just before I wrapped my arms around this particular guy, I threw a wild punch, breaking Tay's nose. Before I knew what was happening, I was down and, for a solid ten minutes, had the stuffing beaten out of me.

From that day on we were friends, but it wasn't until much later in life that we grew to be more like brothers.

Tay and I became Christians at about the same time. After I started attending church, I invited him along. He laughed and made fun of me, but bright and early that Sunday morning he stood outside my apartment door. He had looked almost grim, way too serious for someone going to worship at a church, but I realized he *wanted* to go to church, maybe had wanted to go for a long time, and was taking this visit to the sanctuary quite seriously. I admired his intense focus.

After that first Sunday service together, he apologized for making fun of me. He liked Faith Community Church, but once he told his mother about his new relationship with Jesus, she asked if he would want to attend Rochester Bible Church with her and the rest of the family. As a talented musician, he now leads their worship team and is studying to become a pastor.

As we watched the second half of the game together, I filled him in on all that had been going on.

"And your pastor asked you to look into this?" Tay asked. "Because of what you used to do?"

"Yeah, I suppose." It didn't sound right. "You think he was out of line?"

"Not sure." He had ordered fries and a burger and ate until only crumbs remained. He pressed his fingertips onto the sesame seeds that had fallen off his burger roll onto his plate and sucked them off his fingers.

The photo of Nancy sat on the table between us. Tay shook his head, curled one side of his lips.

"What?" I asked.

"Nothing," he started. "It's just, I've seen your pastor. He's a good-looking guy, and Nancy, well, she's a good-looking woman."

I knew where he was going. "I thought the same thing. But Pastor Ross is married."

"Sure he is. And no one wants to think the pastor of their church could ever do anything wrong, especially not something seriously wrong like adultery."

Adultery. I hated that word. It even sounded dirty and wrong. "Holly's very nice-looking."

"It's not always about looks. I don't think adultery has anything to do with looks. It's about an emptiness one of the partners feels inside—a lacking," he explained. Though his drink was consumed he used his straw and slurped up the remaining drops at the bottom of the glass.

I hated to admit it, but what Tay suggested had crossed my mind. Pastor Ross seemed overly concerned about Nancy. Had there been an affair? Maybe it was even possible that Nancy knew something about Pastor Ross, or had witnessed something, and he was afraid that once away from the church she would tell others about it.

My mind raced. I needed to slow it down. Speculation only leads to trouble. I knew better than that. I needed facts. Facts don't lie.

"You're quite the philosopher, Dr. Brown," I said. "Want another soda, on me?"

"Well, if you put it that way." He smiled.

I picked up our empty glasses and made my way to the bar. As I waited for the barmaid's attention, I watched the television mounted over the bar. The news was on, and the story covered the vandalism at Faith Community Church.

The mo|Ech Prophecy

The scene showed the black spray paint on the church building while the reporter interviewed Gerald Farrar. I tried to listen closely, even though the noise made it difficult to hear.

"We are just as outraged by this shocking display of disrespect as Pastor Ross and his members are, I'm sure," Farrar said. His name was on the screen, and below it read, *Senior Priest of New Forest Church.* I knew the guy looked familiar. He was the priest at the Wiccan church for witches and warlocks just down the road from Faith. "It's a shame that whoever did this unspeakable atrocity chose to incorporate the pentagram in the graffiti. Clearly the pentagram is a symbol of our faith, as the cross is to Christians. Unfortunately, thanks to the likes of Hollywood, an inverted pentagram is immediately associated with witches worshipping Satan. This is simply not true. Satan is a mythological creature created by Christians. We don't believe in God or Satan, so why would we worship Satan?" He laughed, as if linking witches to Satanism was ludicrous. "We follow a simple rule as part of the *Wiccan Rede* and that is 'to harm none.'"

"Is there anything else you'd like to add?" the reporter asked Farrar.

Gerald Farrar looked right into the camera. To me, his eyes resembled smooth, black coal. "Just that we are willing to help Pastor Ross and his members in any way we can, and that, as an equal part of this community, we must stick together to rid the area of all hate crimes."

As I replenished our drinks and made my way back to the booth, a shiver traced its way down my spine. Rather than finding Nancy, I wished Pastor Ross had asked me to look into finding those responsible for defacing our church building.

CHAPTER SEVEN

Earning a buck above minimum wage, I make a humble living as a cook at Phoebe's Diner. Seems like everything in Greece has a way of incorporating Greek Mythology into the business name. Even the high schools are mythological—Athena, Olympia, Arcadia, and Odyssey. Most people don't know Phoebe. For what it's worth, she was Zeus' mother-in-law.

I started about a year ago. It's one of the first legitimate jobs I've ever held. I don't mind making barely enough money to live, because I'm making enough to live. There are things I want but can't afford, so I hold off on buying them. The things I need, God always manages to provide. It's an ongoing process.

With Wednesdays and Sundays off, I work forty-plus hours a week. I usually get to work by five in the morning and leave around four, just before the dinner crowd arrives. I enjoy cracking eggs, whipping up pancakes, and frying omelets. I flame broil burgers and deep-fry fries. The place is pretty busy from six until the time I leave, which is perfect. I don't think I'd be able to handle being bored. Time goes by quickly. Thankfully, I enjoy my job, but work is still work. When my shift ends, I'm always ready to leave.

Normally, I'm not a clock-watcher. Monday morning, though, I had trouble concentrating, burned my hand on the stove while frying an egg, and nicked my finger while dicing an onion. My mind was stuck on Nancy and—I'll admit it—Stacey, and I'll add that my thoughts revolved around my conversation with Tay the previous night.

Was it possible? Could Pastor Ross have been having an affair?

I clocked out, lifted my coat off the hook, and headed out the back door, saying good-bye to the relief cook and one of the waitresses. It never matters how tired I am—when I step out of that back door into fresh air, I just feel rejuvenated.

On Mondays, Wednesdays, and Fridays, after working out at the gym for an hour, I go over to Tay's house. His worship team rehearses in his basement. He plays drums and keyboards. Though I'm not in their group, I do play acoustic guitar. I'm all right; not nearly good enough to play in a band, but they don't mind if I sit in and jam along. So I do, and love every minute of it.

The mo|Ech Prophecy

As I got in and started my car, my cell phone rang. I looked at the display. Stacey. I thought about not answering and letting it roll into my voice mail. I adjusted the heater, increasing the temperature as I flipped open the phone. "Hello?" I said.

"This is Stacey," she said. "We met the other night."

"How are you?" I asked. My car was old. It took forever for the heat to actually blow warm air out of the vents, and in the summer—forget about the air conditioning ever working, I just drove with the windows down.

"Holding up," she said. "You find out anything new?"

"Since last night? No. Nothing." I leaned back, trying to wait patiently for the heater to warm the inside of the car. The temperature had to be dipping into the low thirties. As I breathed I watched wispy, white plumes of breath jet from my mouth. "Look, about this search...."

"You're not giving up, are you?"

I wanted to tell her that, yes, I was thinking about it. I didn't want to be that blunt. It was, after all, Stacey's sister. It wasn't that I didn't think I could find Nancy. I was pretty confident that I could, that I would. I was good at finding people. It was that I didn't want Stacey hounding me night and day. "Not giving up, no. But I've been thinking about this," I said. "Your sister is a grown woman, not a kid, right?"

"So?"

"So, she moved out of her apartment. I talked with the people in the office. She didn't just disappear. She wasn't kidnapped. She moved. Just like the police told my pastor. There's no crime in moving," I said, and noticed the end of an envelope sticking out from my sun visor.

"So you *are* giving up," Stacey said. I could just picture her clenching those long, slender fingers into tight, white-knuckled fists. "I knew it. I knew you'd give up. How long did you look for her anyway? An hour? An afternoon?"

The envelope was addressed to Nancy. I'd forgotten I'd kept it apart from the other mail when I'd handed it over to Stacey. It looked like a bill from a doctor's office. I tipped the envelope this way and that, trying to get a peek inside without tearing it open. Unable to see anything inside, I put it back up in the visor. "Look…."

"Alex Farrar is one of Nancy's best friends. He's not returning any of my calls," she blurted.

"Alex Farrar," I said. The name sounded so familiar. I couldn't place it. "They were close?"

"I don't think like dating-close, but close, yeah."

"You have his phone number?" I asked. I leaned

over and opened my glove box. Tons of junk spilled onto the car floor. I retrieved a pen and scrap of paper, leaving the rest scattered.

"I have his phone number and his address."

"Okay, what is it?" I asked, poising my pen over paper.

"What is what?"

"What is Alex's number and address?" I asked.

"Oh no," she said.

"Oh no, what?"

"You going to see him?"

"Maybe," I said. Why was she making this into a game? "I might just give him a call first."

"He's not answering his phone. I've tried."

"Well, if he has caller ID, he might not be taking calls from you."

There was a silence from her end. Not a dropped call. She was mulling over my point.

"Can we meet?"

"I'm going to be kind of busy," I told her. I didn't want to skip working out. I was getting older. Getting in shape was hard enough, but staying in shape was harder.

"Until when?" she asked.

"Until I'm not busy," I said. "Look, do you want me to keep looking for your sister?"

"Yes. Of course I do."

"Then give me Alex's number and address."

"He's a warlock."

"A what?"

"A warlock. But Nancy always said he was a good warlock."

"Why not? Wendy had a friendly ghost," I mumbled.

"What was that?"

"Nothing." I thought about the news report I'd seen in The Huddle the other day. "Listen, I have something to do until about seven. What if we meet for coffee around then?" I suggested.

"Seven? That sounds good. Where?"

"There's a place called Java Brew in the plaza over on Dewey and Latta," I said. "You know it?"

"I'll meet you there at seven. Coffee's on me this time."

"Fair enough. I'll see you then." I ended the call.

I rubbed my hands together. The friction created some warmth. Not enough. I was going to have to drive with gloves on.

A warlock. What had Stacey's sister gotten herself into?

CHAPTER EIGHT

After a solid one-hour workout, I drove over to Tay's. He lived in the city in a four-bedroom colonial off Chili Avenue—pronounced *chie-lie*, not *chill-ee*. Go figure. Only the color used to paint or side each of the homes distinguished one residence from the next. The neighborhood always seemed quiet and peaceful. I knew Tay's basement was soundproof, but I wondered if his band's rehearsals weren't heard above and beyond those cement block walls.

I parked, took my guitar case out of the trunk, walked up to Tay's porch, and rang the bell.

"Who is it?" Tay called out from inside. "Tommy?"

"Yeah, it's me!"

"Come on in. Coke's in the fridge."

I loved his home: polished, hardwood floors, gumwood trim, large rooms with high ceilings. I moved through the family room and dining room into the kitchen, grabbed a cold soda, and went down into the basement.

Aside from the sight of a furnace, hot-water heater, washer, dryer, and some baskets of—hopefully—clean laundry, the basement resembled a mini recording studio. Green indoor-outdoor carpeting covered the plain cement floor, while rectangular sections of egg carton foam hung on the walls to absorb sound. In one corner of the room sat a rather large, burgundy drum set, surrounded by so many symbols it resembled an invasion of flying saucers. Microphone stands stood in a semicircle in the center of the room, with another by an electric keyboard a few feet from the drum set.

In the background were a mixing board and amplifiers—big, black amplifiers. A couple of guitars—one electric, one acoustic-electric—stood in stands by some of the amps. Last, the floor looked as if it was crawling with black snakes, coiled and ready to strike; but these were the guitar and microphone cords running in all directions, stuffed into inputs and outputs all over the place. I didn't even pretend to understand how everything worked. I just enjoyed the atmosphere it all created.

I opened my case, put the strap over my neck, sat on one of the many flat, wooden barstools, and tuned my guitar.

"You're a bit early," Tay said, coming down the basement stairs, a soda and drumsticks in hand.

"But that's cool. We can jam together for awhile. What do you say?"

"Chris Tomlin?" I suggested. Tomlin was one of my favorite artists, not because most of his songs were easy to play on guitar but because most of his songs really made an impact in my life.

Tay sat behind the drum set, clicked his sticks four times to begin, and, for what seemed like a blissful eternity, we played "How Great Is Our God." Tay sang. His voice was strong, powerful. I could not carry a tune to save my life. But I played, strumming away as if my life depended on it.

"That was something," Tay said. "You're really getting good. I mean, really good."

I thought I'd sounded all right, but I'd never admit it—not to a musician as talented as Tay. "I'm working on it," I said, my modest reply. I set the guitar down and opened a Coke.

"So what's bothering you?" Tay asked.

"Pretty obvious, huh?"

He shrugged. "You're my brother, man. I can read you all right."

I told him about the call from Stacey.

"So this secretary hangs out with a warlock?" Tay said. He shook his head and pursed his lips. He used the tip of a drumstick to scratch his back.

"That's what Stacey said."

"And it's, who? Farrar? Gerald Farrar?"

Gerald was the Wiccan priest from New Forest Church. I had thought the name *Farrar* sounded familiar. "No," I said. "Stacey said his name was Alex Farrar."

"Like Gerald's son?"

"I don't know. I don't even know if Gerald has a son. I mean, I was thinking about just walking away from this. I have no idea what Pastor Ross is really looking for. And you know what? It doesn't really concern me."

"I agree with you. I told you I thought he might be out of line coming to you with this in the first place," Tay said. "Want to play another song before the rest of the band gets here?"

"I'd—do you mind if I use your computer real quick?" I asked.

"See if you can find this Alex Farrar?"

"Yeah."

"I'd let you, but Leatrice has it. She's upgrading it with all kinds of memory and sound boards and a million other things," he said. He pounded out a drumroll on his snare and topped it off with a crash from one of his symbols.

"Nice to be dating a computer geek," I teased.

"Hey, watch it," Tay said, smiling. "So you're not walking away from this?" He twirled a drumstick in his fingers absently as he took a long, draining swig from his can of soda.

The mol**Ech** Prophecy

"Look at it this way, Tay: Alex has to be related to Gerald. Stacey said he was a warlock. What are the chances? So my guess is that he attends New Forest. This whole thing went from seemingly senseless to suddenly peculiar," I said.

"I love that word, man. *Peculiar.* The word even sounds...peculiar, don't you think?" He laughed, cleared his throat, and then sat up straight when he saw I was serious. "Oh, sorry, what were you saying? What's peculiar?"

"About a week or so ago, Nancy Callahan stops coming to work. She moves out of her apartment. She clearly moves out. Nobody seems to see anything odd there, at least not the police, and I agree, nothing's really odd. I mean, she wasn't taken in the middle of the night. She actually gathered up her things and left."

"I'm with you so far," Tay said, leaning forward, showing his interest.

"Sometime yesterday, before the church service, our building is defaced with satanic symbols and hateful, godless graffiti," I explained. "And then last night I see Gerald Farrar on television, expressing his sympathy. Now I learn that maybe Nancy is best friends with this priest's son."

"Man, that is peculiar," Tay said, smiling like a simpleton. "You think everything ties together?"

I did. It started to make me a little nervous.

"Looks that way," I said. "But you want to know what scares me the most right now?"

"What's that?"

"Where does Pastor Ross fit into all of this?" I asked. People would be arriving any minute for practice. I knew there wasn't time for Tay and me to flesh things out. Right now, this was something Ross had asked me to do. It wasn't that it was a tough task. I could find Nancy. It was just a, well, peculiar task. "You mind if I bail?"

"Getting back in the saddle, man?" Tay asked. He wasn't smiling. He knew who I had been before I became a new man in Christ. We had been the same for too many years. Neither of us ever wanted to consider what would happen if we started backsliding.

"This time it's not for money, man. It's not like that," I said. I tried to flash a reassuring grin, but I had a bad taste in the back of my throat—like vomit, but I strongly suspected it was just my past attempting to crawl back up out of the depths of my gut, looking for oxygen to breathe life back into its unwanted soul.

"I know it's not, Tommy. You need me, I'm here. Know what I'm saying?"

"You got my back," I verified.

"Always," he said. "You still gonna take off?

"Yeah. I've got to do some digging, you know?"

The mo|Ech Prophecy

We punched fists over one of his tom-toms. "I'll be in touch."

"Before you go, you mind if we pray? Warlocks and everything, that's some serious stuff. I don't want you digging around out there all alone," Tay said.

"I'd love it." We bowed our heads and Tay led us in a prayer for protection.

Chapter Nine

Since I didn't have to meet Stacey until seven*ish* at Java Brew, I decided to swing by the church. I wanted photos of the graffiti. When I got there, the parking lot was empty.

I took my digital camera out of the glove box and climbed out of the car. It was dark, like midnight. November clouds blocked the stars and moon from view. A few light poles spaced intermittently throughout the lot lit shining halos on the four parking spaces below each pole, but little else was visible.

I took several pictures of the graffiti from different angles far away, and then moved closer to take individual shots of each obscenity and hateful symbol. Deciding to inspect the entire church, I walked slowly around the property. Without a flashlight, it was tough to see if anything else had been sprayed on the building. As far as I could tell, all the defacing had been done in front.

I took a few steps away from the back of the

church and snapped another picture just to be certain I wasn't missing anything. I studied the image on the camera display and confirmed nothing had been added to the back walls when I heard the distinct sound of a shell being pumped into a rifle barrel.

Instinctively, my hands raised slowly into the air even before I heard a man's voice say, "Turn around."

"I'm going to turn around real slow," I said. I wanted whoever it was to know I was not going to try anything funny. True to my word, I took baby steps as I rotated myself one hundred and eighty degrees. "I don't want any trouble," I said calmly.

"What's that in your hands?" he asked. I could not see his face, or much of anything. His form, like a living shadow, clearly held a weapon of some sort—and that weapon was unmistakably pointed in my direction.

"My camera."

"You a reporter?" he asked.

"I go to church here."

"So you came back to get pictures of your disgusting artwork!" The man sounded angry.

This made me nervous. I didn't need some unsteady guy pointing his gun at me. The last time someone pointed a gun at me, I knew he'd meant to shoot and kill me. He'd hesitated. I had taken advantage of that hesitation, grabbing the gun from his hand and beating him unconscious with it. I'd honestly believed that time was the last time I'd find myself in a situation where a gun was being pointed at me. Guess I'd been mistaken.

"Wasn't me," I said. I didn't want to explain everything to him about Nancy, Stacey, and New Forest Church. It was too complicated. Right now simplicity was the answer. "I'm just taking photos."

"You some kind of a photographer?"

"Sure," I said. "Pastor Ross has me looking into this." I nodded my head toward the church.

"You're not one of them?" he asked.

The headlights from a car passing by on Latta Road gave just enough light for me to see the man in front of me. He looked like a farmer in a plaid, flannel coat. Under a John Deere baseball cap were wisps of white and gray hair. His white T-shirt was visible under his barely buttoned, dingy, yellow dress shirt. He wore faded blue jeans and construction boots.

The fleeting light allowed the darkness to surround us once again.

"One of *who*?" Silence stood between us. "One of who?" I asked a second time.

"I don't always see them when they're here, but

they come at night—not like now, but late, late at night," he said.

"You know who did this spray painting?" I asked.

"I didn't see who did that blasphemous thing, no sir. But I suspect it was them," he said.

"And who are they?"

"I can't say for certain. I think they live back there, deep in the woods," the man said. He never lowered his gun. It remained pointed directly at me. I prayed his finger wasn't resting on the trigger as well. And while I was at it, I prayed the safety was on, too.

A jumbled mess of questions clogged my brain. *What people? How many people? How often did he see them? When was the first time he saw them? When was the last time he saw them? Are they just men? Are there women? Are they just women? Are they teenagers?* And last, *Is this guy just some loon who happens to live close by?*

"Can we go around front and talk where it's light?" I asked.

"Can't. They'll see me."

"Who will?"

"Them. The people back in the woods."

I got the distinct feeling that this man was afraid. He didn't want to be seen, and yet here he was, armed with a rifle and hanging around on church property.

"The church owns acres and acres around here," I said. "More than likely the woods you're talking about are owned by the church. If people really are living back there, they're trespassing, at the very least."

He said nothing.

"Is that where you live, right up by Latta?" It was a big, white colonial, the church's nearest neighbor. If he did indeed live there, then the woods the church owned butted up against the property he owned, as well.

"You better get going," the man said.

"Sir, sir. Have you talked with the people from the woods?"

"It's not safe. If they see me here, talking with you, then it's not safe," he said. He started backing up, headed toward Latta, toward the white colonial. He kept the gun trained on me, though.

"Safe for who, sir? For me? For you? Have they threatened you?" I questioned.

"If you say you're working for Pastor Ross, then get going. Get out of here, go on." He shooed me away with a wave of the barrel of his rifle.

"Have you told the police about them?"

He stopped his retreat. "Once. That's how I know they'll be very, very upset if they see me talking with you," he said. I could hear fear in his trembling voice. He'd been threatened. After he'd talked with the police, they must have warned him about never doing it again.

"My name's Tommy," I offered.

"Tommy, I'm not going to say it again—get out of here." He begged, pleading with me to leave. "I shouldn't have even come out tonight. But I saw you pull into the parking lot. I saw you get out of your car and then I saw you sneaking around. It's not my job to protect this place. No one asked me to watch over this church. What was I thinking?"

The brave man who came out here with a rifle hoping to catch a criminal had now backed away from me so quickly I couldn't help wonder where he had rounded up the courage in the first place.

At least I was right about one thing: the white colonial belonged to him. I watched as he made his way back to the house, stepping out of the darkness and into light cast by the streetlights and the light coming from his home. Occasionally he stole a glance toward the woods. *Could people be just beyond the trees, watching us?* It didn't seem likely, and yet the hairs on my arms and on the back of my neck stood up and my skin tingled.

I jogged back around to the front of the church and climbed into my car. From where I sat, I thought

Thomas Phillips

I saw the old man looking out from a window. As I strained to see better, the lights in his house went out.

My throat felt extremely dry as I started up the engine. I locked my camera away in the glove box and pulled out of the parking lot onto Latta Road.

It was almost seven. It was time to meet Stacey at Java Brew.

CHAPTER TEN

Java Brew was a small coffeehouse in a small eight-store shopping plaza, sandwiched between a bowling supply store and an Italian deli. There were plenty of free parking spaces, so spotting Stacey was easy. Though it was five to seven, she stood, leaning against her dark blue car with arms crossed, as if I'd kept her waiting for hours.

I parked next to her. "Hey," I said when I got out of the car.

"That your guitar?" she asked.

I smiled. "Yep," I said as I took it out of the back seat and placed it in the trunk. "Been here long?"

She looked at her watch: "Two minutes."

"You looked angry when I pulled in."

She wrinkled her nose. "Did I?" She shrugged. "I was just thinking, I guess."

"About Nancy?"

She smiled. "Let's get coffee, then we'll talk."

She turned and walked toward the front entrance, several steps ahead of me. I felt like I should be carrying shopping bags for her or something. We walked into Java Brew and ordered. I let Stacey pay. We took seats at a small table for two near the back.

Though it seemed a bit over the top, white Christmas lights wrapped and outlined nearly everything in the place. Java Brew was not very large but it seemed like there was plenty of space, despite being packed full of bookracks, magazines on coffee tables, sofas, chairs, and tables.

"They have open mike night here on Wednesdays," Stacey said. She shrugged out of her coat and hung it over the back of her chair. "You going to stay awhile?"

"I like to keep my coat on," I said.

"Because it makes you look cool?" she teased as she sat down.

"Does it?" I said, ogling and feeling the leather as if for the first time. I sat down, too. "I suppose it does."

She laughed. I liked her laugh. It was a little deep, but soft. "I bet I could get the owner to let you play us a few songs right now if you want." She played an air guitar.

I laughed. "I don't think so," I said.

"Come on. What are you? Shy?"

"I play for me," I said.

"You any good?"

The mo‌Ech Prophecy

"I play all right," I said, maybe bragging a little to show off. "I'm okay. I haven't been playing long."

"Modest."

"Not really."

"Right. I think you're just being modest," she said, stirring her coffee with a stir stick.

"Just being honest," I insisted.

"You sing?"

"That is the last thing you want, believe me. You do not want me singing," I promised. "I can't carry a tune at all."

"I doubt you're *that* bad," she said.

I sipped my coffee. It was too hot to drink. I set the cup back down. "One day I wouldn't mind sitting on stage at church and just playing rhythm guitar for the worship band, you know? Kind of in the background of it all," I said. I could not believe I was doing the talking. When I looked up at Stacey, she seemed a little taken aback that I'd just opened up, too.

"What do you do for a living?" I asked.

She eyed me suspiciously, but the half-smile she displayed told me my question was appropriate enough. "I'm a real estate agent."

I didn't really have a follow-up question. I was just making conversation, but I was also trying to take the attention off of me.

She laughed. "Kind of boring, I know."

"No, not at all," I said. "How long have you been doing that?"

"Five years. It's a pretty good business here," she said. "I research the market, help people find what they're looking for, sell what they don't want, and spend Sundays doing open houses."

After a few more minutes of small talk, I said, "All right. I guess we need to get down to business. Tell me about Alex Farrar."

"What's going on?" she asked. She looked suddenly serious.

I let out a quick laugh. "What are you talking about?"

"Did you find something out?"

"Are you playing games with me?" I asked. I could feel my face getting warm. Not burning, but warm.

"What do you mean?"

"It's like every time we talk you're playing a game. You want me to help, but you won't give me everything at once. I have to work to get information from you. Like coming here—you could have given me Farrar's number and address over the phone. We didn't have to meet for coffee," I said, talking through clenched teeth.

My temper. I tried to keep it in check. I took a deep breath and sighed. "Look, I'm sorry."

The ~~molEch~~ Prophecy

She shook her head.

"I'm sorry," I said again.

She tried to smile, and when it failed, she looked away. "I still think you found out something else," she insisted. "And you're the one playing games. You're the one not telling me everything. I don't know you. I don't know if I can trust you."

"And I know you?" I said.

"You know I'm Nancy's sister. That should be enough for you to trust me," she said. "But I know this about you—you're holding back. You've found out something else, haven't you?"

Laughing again, I leaned back in the chair and rested my hands on my thighs. "Why do you say that?"

"When we were talking on the phone, you were about to tell me you were done, that you weren't going to spend another second looking for my sister," she said.

She was right. I was going to keep looking, but she didn't know that.

"But as soon as I mentioned that Nancy's friend was a warlock, something in your tone changed. It was more than just curiosity. For some reason I believe that Alex Farrar is the reason you haven't given up," she said.

This time she was only partially right. Alex Farrar was the reason she was still in the loop.

"Let's start this over, all right? I'll tell you what I know, you tell me what you know. And I promise to keep looking, but only until I think there's nothing else I can do," I said. "Sometimes, no matter how hard we look, some people don't want to be found. So what do you say? We have a deal?"

She held out her hand.

"One more thing," I said, staring at her long, slender fingers. "After today, I'm doing this on my own."

She pulled her hand back. "What if you need my help?"

"I won't."

"But if you do?"

"I won't."

"But if you do?" She was relentless.

"Then I'll call you."

"That's all I'm asking." She held out her hand. I shook it.

"Now tell me about Alex Farrar," I said.

Chapter Eleven

It was just after eight when we stepped out of Java Brew. As we walked slowly toward our cars, I couldn't help noticing Stacey's smile. She talked about a time when she and Nancy went fishing with their father. Both under ten, they'd rowed a boat out to the center of a pond. When their dad opened a Styrofoam container full of dirt, she and Nancy peered in expectantly. Never having fished before, they laughed when they saw the thick worms. They laughed until their dad showed them how to really secure a worm in place on a hook.

"Worm guts sprayed all over the place," she laughed, pressing a hand to her chest as if to control the outburst. "Nancy got so scared, or grossed out, or whatever, that she jumped up to her feet. The boat rocked off balance, and she and I both fell in the water."

I laughed, picturing Stacey as a young girl falling in a large pond, screaming and splashing. Despite my laughter, my eyes never left her, studying her face. Her skin looked so silky, so soft. Her green eyes shined, reflecting the light beaming down from the light pole we stood under. Her lips looked so red, so full.

"You know, it's getting kind of late," I said, looking at my watch. "And I've completely skipped dinner...."

Her laugh abruptly stopped, and that smile I'd been so intently studying immediately lost its shape. "I'm sorry, I didn't mean to keep you," she said. She pulled car keys out of her purse.

"No, that's not what I meant," I said. I shook my head, smiling.

"What?"

"I was wondering if you maybe wanted to grab something to eat with me?" I said. When she lowered her chin but continued to look up at me, I felt something inside me stir. "Nothing fancy. I was just going to head over to Phoebe's for a burger and fries." I didn't have much money. Since I was an employee, I got 50 percent off the bill when I ate there. And I ate there regularly. It was often cheaper than grocery shopping.

"Yeah, sure. That sounds good," she said. "I'll follow you."

The mo‖Ech Prophecy

What I loved most about Phoebe's was the family atmosphere. Dominic was a great boss. He'd owned the place forever. He treated everyone like a close personal friend. And not only did the waitresses know most people by name, but they also knew, pretty much, what each regular intended to order. At a minimum, they would bring over a drink of choice without the customer ordering it. Nothing about the place stood out; it had bland colors, booths on the outside, tables in the middle, and a long L-shaped counter for diners who preferred a spinning bar stool.

"I've never been here," Stacey whispered.

"I work here," I said.

"Hey, Tommy," Kali said. "Table for two?"

"How about a booth, Kali?" I suggested.

She smiled warmly and led us to a corner. "How's this?"

"Perfect," I said. "This is Stacey, a friend of mine."

They shook hands.

"Can I bring you coffee?"

I was coffeed out. "A Coke for me," I said.

"Diet Coke, please," Stacey said.

She handed us menus. I didn't need one but took one anyway. "I'll be right back with the Cokes; give you a chance to see what you want."

"Thanks," I said as she turned and walked away.

"She's cute," Stacey said.

"My friend Tay—the musician I told you about? He's seeing her mother. The three of them go to church together. Her mother works for the church as their computer tech person."

"That's nice," she said. "She seems like a nice kid."

"Hard worker, too," I said. "She's been a waitress here for nearly a year. She's a senior in high school, has missed out on sports, school events, and social parties because she works nearly every night. She wants to go to college next fall. Her parents are divorced. Her father has plenty of money but already told her there'll be no free rides. She lives with her mother. Since her grades will never land her a scholarship, she's determined to pay tuition costs on her own without asking her father for a cent."

"That's pretty admirable," she said.

"When I was that age, school was the last thing on my mind," I said.

After ordering, we filled the time before the food came with small talk.

"So you work here, huh? What do you do?" She asked.

"I'm a cook."

The mo|Ech Prophecy

"I can't cook a thing," she said. "I mean, I can make things like oatmeal—using the microwave—but outside of that, microwave cooking, I'm at a loss. How'd you get into cooking? I mean, your pastor asked you to find my sister. If he knows you're a cook—and I don't mean anything negative by that—but if he knows you're a cook, why ask you?"

"Your parents still married? Were they ever?" I asked, not so subtly.

She let out a little laugh that was more like a grunt. "You don't want to talk to me?"

"Sure I do."

"Just not about yourself," she said. It wasn't a question.

"Not much to tell."

"You mean, nothing you want to share. Everyone has a story to tell."

"I have nothing to hide," I said.

"Then answer the question. Why would a pastor ask a cook to try and find a missing person?" She stared at me. Her eyes looked like emeralds—big, dark, shiny, captivating.

Kali showed up with our drinks. "Food will be out shortly, okay?"

"Thanks, Kali," I said, giving her a wink.

Stacey was just staring at me, waiting.

"It's a long story," I said to Stacey once Kali walked away.

She looked at her watch. "It's not even eight thirty. You have a curfew or something?"

Chapter Twelve

"It really started about ten years ago. I was sixteen," I said. I stared at my hands, which played with the straw wrapper, rolling it into a ball and then unrolling it....

Tay sat on a swing, his arms wrapped around the chains; a lit cigarette dangled from his lip and his head hung low, watching while his toes traced meaningless patterns in the oval of dirt under his feet. So much cigarette smoke rose up around his head that it seemed like his brain was on fire.

"Man, are they coming, or what?" I asked. I had smoked my cigarette to the filter but used it to light another before flicking the first out into the grass. It had to be almost midnight. Tay and I were dressed similarly. While he wore a white tank top, mine was black. We both had on baggy blue jeans and black biker boots.

"Said he'd be here," Tay said. He dropped his cigarette onto the ground and then kicked dirt over it.

Trevor "Bones" White should have been at the park an hour ago. I was getting tired of waiting. I climbed up and sat on top of the monkey bars. "Bones say how much we get?"

"It's a percent," Tay said. "It all works on percentages."

"Like I pay attention in math," I said. I saw headlights turn off the main road into the parking lot. "He say what the percent is?"

"He didn't," Tay said, standing up. "Let's not worry about it."

"But don't you want to know?"

"Bones isn't going to want to talk about it," Tay said. "Leave it alone for now, got it?"

Bones worked for King. No one knew King's name for sure. As best I could tell, except for Bones, no one even knew what King looked like. He was like a legend.

"Should we go to the car?" I asked. I couldn't sit still. I slipped down between the bars, dangled for a moment, and then dropped to my feet.

"Bones said he'd meet us by the swings. We stay here," Tay said.

"Sure, whatever."

The mo**Ech** Prophecy

I heard a car door open, only one door, but because the headlights were still on I couldn't see anything until a lone shadow of a man stepped in front of the car. The light was almost blinding as it shone all around him. It resembled something out of a dream.

"What's up, boys?" Bones said. He and Tay did a ritualistic handshake, then hugged. Though they were both black, Bones' skin looked at least a hundred shades darker than Tay's. The whites of his eyes seemed to glow, surrounded by the blackness of his skin. "Tommy, man, what's new?" he asked, going through the handshake and hug with me.

"Not much," I managed. "But, Bones, I got a question."

Tay backhanded my arm.

"Yo, quit it," I said, threatening to pop him in the arm with my cocked fist.

"What's on your mind, Tommy?" Bones asked. He pulled a pack of cigarettes from his pocket. Tay lit his Zippo and offered up the flame.

"Now that Tay and I work for you and the King, what's our percentage? I mean, all I keep hearing is I'll get a percentage of everything, you know. That don't help me figure nothing out, though, not when I haven't got a clue what percent I can count on," I said.

Tay chewed on his lower lip. He looked embarrassed, agitated. "Tommy, man," he said.

"Nah, it's cool. It's cool. Man's got hisself a fair question," Bones said. He took a long drag on the cigarette. As he blew smoke from his mouth and nostrils, he said, "Eight percent."

I nodded. That sounded all right.

"To split," added Bones.

"Four percent each?" I asked. I stood a little taller, felt the muscles in my arms tense a bit. "We split the 8 percent between us?"

"That's right," Bones said. "You got a problem with that?"

I did have a problem with 4 percent.

"You think you start at the top? You think, maybe you should get half?" Bones yelled. "You think the King is getting rich and you're getting the short end of the shaft?"

I wanted to yell, *Yeah, that's exactly what I think!*

Bones settled down, taking a deep breath, leaning against the swing set frame. "Look at it this way, boys. Say you break into a store and get away with a couple of radios, all right? What you think King's going to do with more radios? They aren't worth anything to him. He's got to find someone to unload the stuff. Someone's got to sell the radios. That someone's got to get a percent of the sale, too, no? Sometimes there's so much junk coming in that King has to find places to put all the loot. Well, there go more percents, if you see what I'm saying. By the time the whole pie is sliced and diced, King's not getting a piece much bigger than yours. Is it bigger? Sure it's bigger. He's the boss, man. He's the boss."

"Four percent's cool," I said.

Both Tay and Bones smiled.

"That's what I like to hear, man. I knew you was good, Tommy. King's been watching you since you were going to brawls in that little street gang of yours," Bones said.

"I'm done with the gang," I said.

"Which is exactly why King likes you," Bones said. "And you, too, Tay. It's exactly why he's excited to have you working for him."

"So when do we start earning that 4 percent?" I asked.

Bones smiled. I'd thought the whites of his eyes were white, but his teeth were like polished snow. Maybe it was where he got his nickname.

"The stuff is in two bags in the grass in front of where I parked. One for each of you. In each bag, the stuff is divided up into a hundred sample packets. You give these away," Bones said.

"We *give the drugs away*," I said. "And where does my 4 percent come from on that? I'm not great in math or nothing, but 4 percent of zero is zero."

He moved like lightening. His hand clapped around the back of my neck. His fingers were like knives digging into my flesh. The pain came quickly, and it was intense. I dropped to my knees, my eyes shut—I couldn't have opened them if I'd wanted to.

"I've entertained your rudeness long enough, don't you think? That mouth of yours, that brain, it's going to get you into some serious, serious trouble, man."

Bones did not let up but instead applied more pressure. He wanted to hear me scream. I didn't want to scream. Unable to bear any more, I let out a groan that grew into a cry. Bones squeezed harder still, then threw me forward, finally letting go. My eyes teared up and saw things in a blur. Curled up on the ground, I tried to roll my head around to relieve some of the pain in my neck. It didn't work.

"May I finish?" Bones asked, but he wasn't really asking.

"Please," I said. I closed my eyes tight. Talking hurt. The inside of my skull throbbed. I pulled myself up onto my knees.

"The free bags is what gets 'em hooked. When they come back for more, and they will, then you start charging them," Bones said. "There's money

The molEch Prophecy

to be made here, boys. Big money. More than you teenyboppers ever dreamed."

I was counting on it. Money was something I desperately needed.

Chapter Thirteen

Kali brought out our orders. Stacey and I had ordered burgers, fries, and coleslaw. "Refill on the sodas? You had the diet?" she confirmed, pointing at Stacey.

"Right," Stacey said.

Stacey snagged one of my fries. "Whoa—you have your own," I said.

Kali returned a second later with refills.

As we ate, I waited for Stacey to say something, anything, about the story I'd just told. "Don't you have anything to say?" I asked.

"About what?"

"About what? About what I just told you?" I said.

"You want me to believe you sold drugs?"

"You think I made it up?" I asked.

She shook her head. "So you're telling me that your pastor asked you to help find my sister because you were in a gang and became a teenage drug pusher?"

The molEch Prophecy

"There's more," I said. There's always more. "After two years of selling drugs, I guess King and Bones had other plans for me...."

Bones stood outside a bar on Genesee Street. He leaned against the bricks, smoking a cigarette. I walked toward him, hands in my pockets—one gripped a switchblade. *Trust no one* was the philosophy I lived by—no one, that is, except maybe Tay.

When I was close enough, Bones stood up straight. We shook hands and hugged. "So what's up?" I said. Bones and I had seen each other nearly every week for the last few years. Not once did he ever call and ask for me to meet him anywhere public. We always met in parks and back lots. So when he had called my cell that morning asking me to meet him over by Charlie's on Genesee, I couldn't help feeling nervous.

"King wants to see you," he said.

This did nothing to settle my nerves. King was a legend, a myth. I'd stopped believing long ago that the royal man even existed. He'd become like Santa Claus and the Tooth Fairy. I'd even begun to assume that Bones was really King, that Bones used King as a way to earn respect, a means to induce supernatural fear.

"Me? Why?" I asked. I was conscious of the switchblade in my pocket. I'd pulled it many times. I'd cut a kid's face once. I was not afraid to kill, especially if it was in self-defense.

"Relax, man. You're not in any trouble," Bones said.

"I'm not?" I asked.

"Should you be?" Bones asked, suspiciously.

"No. No way." I looked around. "So where is he?"

"He's inside, man. He's waiting."

We walked into Charlie's. Inside was dark. It took awhile for my eyes to adjust. Cigarette and cigar smoke filled the place. Obviously, people at Charlie's didn't care much if it was against the law to smoke indoors.

The bar along the wall on the left was well lit. A rectangular lamp, surrounded by stained glass, hung from the ceiling over a billiards table. Every other nook and cranny was barely illuminated by low-wattage lighting.

"He's back here," Bones said, leading the way. "You carrying?"

"Not a gun," I said. "I've got a switchblade."

"Turn it over, man," he said.

I reluctantly handed it to Bones. "I want that back."

He laughed. He showed me the butt of a Glock

sticking out of the waistband of his pants. "Not interested in your utensils."

Sitting directly in front of me was King. He had a table to himself. He sat with his back to the wall, allowing him to see everything that went on in the bar. To his right—my left—stood a door clearly marked EXIT in red letters. King's back-way out.

When I thought there might be a King, I pictured someone completely different from the man now sitting before me.

"King, this here's Tommy," Bones said.

I held out my hand. He did not shake it.

This white man had to be fifty, maybe sixty. He had a thick head of silver hair, peppered with streaks of black. He wore a black suit, white shirt, no tie. Gold necklaces, large-jeweled rings, and a Rolex radiated success. A short, fat cigar dangled from his lips. He chewed the end, wrinkling his mouth to move the stogie from one side to the other and back again. "Sit down," said the King. "I got a job for you."

I expected small talk; maybe he'd tell me that Bones had told him what a good worker I was, or we'd discuss how well I ran my territory. I thought he might ask me questions about sales, the cops, or about his relationships with the junkies he'd turned on to crack. The stock market, the weather, something, but there was no small talk at all. I kept my mouth shut and just nodded.

"People owe me money. Lots of people. I need a couple of guys I can trust who can track down these people and collect for me," he said. "Bones tells me you know how to handle yourself."

I nodded, again, but just a slight nod. I wanted to project coolness.

King seemed satisfied. "But I need a team that has some brains. A team that can make executive decisions and not call me every ten minutes for my input."

"But if you make a wrong choice," Bones interjected, "it'll be your fault."

I swallowed. "I get what you're saying."

"You get what he's saying?" King asked.

I nodded.

"So King sends you after Fatty Frank who's into us for two grand. King wants his money, all of it, right now. So you track Fatty down, and say you find him holed up in some dump, but all he's got is a grand, what do you do?"

"I take the grand, I beat him good, and tell him I'll be back in three days for the rest," I said quickly, confidently.

"You don't force him to give you the other grand?"

"Can't get blood from a stone, is the way I see

it. The grand's a good start, and three days is just that—three days."

King stared at me for what seemed like hours—but in reality it was more like seconds—before laughing. "You see? That's what I'm talking about. That's what I'm looking for, Tommy. You're like a natural, or something," King said, holding out his hand.

I shook it, knowing I'd just moved up the ranks a few rungs. I wanted to ask about money. What would my cut be? Would it still be four percent, or what? Instead, I kept silent. Bones winked at me. I think he knew percentages were running through my mind and he was clearly relieved I didn't open my mouth with insulting questions.

We'd finished eating. Stacey just stared at me, both her hands lightly gripping her Diet Coke. "You're not kidding around with me, are you? You're part of a gang?"

"Was."

"And you sell drugs?"

"Sold."

"And you found people and beat them up because they owed some guy money?"

"Used to," I reminded her. "Tay and I both did.

We were partnered up. But I don't do that anymore. I haven't in years."

"Years? Like, two or three?"

"Almost four," I countered.

"So, you know how to find people?"

"I was pretty good at it, yeah."

"Did you have to find a lot of people?" she asked.

"All the time."

"Were there people you couldn't find?"

"I found them all eventually," I told her.

Speechless, she sipped her soda. "So, what about all of this being a religious fanatic? How did that come about?"

Normally, I enjoyed the opportunity to share my testimony. I wanted to tell Stacey about me, but right now I needed more time. The last few years I've spent most of my time cleaning myself up, focusing my attention on God. A woman in my life was the last thing I wanted or needed. But now, I felt something for Stacey. She wasn't a Christian. The Bible warns about being unequally yoked. Dating someone who didn't share my faith or love for Jesus would put immediate stress on the relationship.

"That's another story," I told her, "for another time."

"Will you tell it to me?"

The mol̶E̶ch Prophecy

"I will, but not tonight."

She regarded me with a slight nod. "But you will tell me."

"I promise," I said.

Chapter Fourteen

I lived in a small one-bedroom apartment complete with a tiny kitchenette and couch with a pullout mattress. My television sat on a stand next to the stereo in front of the couch. Next to my closet by the back window was a small desk just large enough to house my computer stuff. I sat at the desk in a folding chair and logged on to the Internet.

New Forest Church had its own Web site, which is what I expected. What I didn't expect was the overall brightness of the site. I thought for sure the background would be black with blood-red lettering. I imagined daggers and ram skulls with coiled horns for icons.

Instead, there was a photo of a smiling Gerald Farrar. With gray hair, blue eyes, and white teeth, the priest looked friendly and welcoming. The tab bar allowed me to tour the Web site and learn more about the church. I found dates and times of services, directions to the church, background about the origins of the church in our area, information about their worship team, photos from their youth group events, a brief biography of Farrar, a calendar of upcoming events, and a special password-protected tab for church members only.

I sat back in my chair and crossed my arms. This church Web site did not look much different from Faith's Web site. I found it hard to believe that Wiccans would have a youth group, but it made sense. Parents who were Wiccans would want their kids reared in the ways of Wicca as well, I suppose.

But there were three tabs that I did not recognize. One said "The 8 Sabbats," another said "Magick," and the third odd tab said "Wiccan Rede."

I clicked on the "Wiccan Rede" tab and learned that the members of New Forest were known as a coven instead of a congregation, and that the *Rede* was their law. Much like the Ten Commandments, the *Rede* governed Wiccan behavior, warning those in the coven that the main rule to live by is that they *harm none*. This was what Farrar had talked about during his news interview on Sunday.

Wiccans also believe in something called the "Threefold Law," so that any harm or good a warlock puts on someone else will come back on him as a blessing or a curse, magnified three times over.

Apparently, Wiccans did not consider themselves to be satanists, or even warlocks and witches, like I would have thought. They worship multiple gods and goddesses but apparently not the devil. Call me ignorant, but I really didn't see much difference. As far as I was concerned, the worship of anything or anyone other than the one true God was inspired by Satan.

Next, I clicked on the worship tab and scrolled down toward the bottom of the page. There was a picture of a young man with straight, shoulder-length brown hair. He did not smile and had thin lips. His best feature was a pair of big brown eyes. Under the picture was his name: Alex Farrar. Gerald's son? Nancy's friend. He was the church's worship leader, and a guitar player, no less.

I'll admit, my curiosity was piqued most by the password-protected area of the Web site. Maybe they had things like people's phone numbers and addresses that they didn't want to have published publicly online. Or maybe there was other hidden information altogether.

As I looked more closely at each page of the site, I was amazed by the huge amounts of information. I had no idea that there were dozens of covens in Rochester alone. I didn't realize that pagans put their faith in a number of gods, while witches and warlocks put their faith in magic. Not all pagans were Wiccan, and not all Wiccans were pagans.

They met in churches, like the one where New Forest was housed, but they preferred meeting outdoors. As I looked at photos on the Web site, I found many disturbing and unnatural images. A few showed different angles of a coven of witches and warlocks decked out in hunter green or dark robes, holding hands, and encircling a blazing bonfire.

Apparently, they spent a lot of time studying the phases of the moon: waxing, full, waning, dark, and new. Their seasons determined when they would practice particular rituals known as Sabbats, and any time a ritual was performed outside of a Sabbat, it was known as an Esbat.

During the week, New Forest offered classes for new witches and warlocks. Wednesday classes were entitled *Getting Started the Wiccan Way*. Classes were offered for witches and warlocks at all different levels of spell casting, tapestry weaving, tarot card reading, and psychic enhancing.

There was too much to take in.

I took some notes and jotted down what time the church was meeting this coming Saturday evening.

It was getting late. I had to be up early for work in the morning. Before getting ready for bed I called Tay on my cell phone.

"Am I waking you?" I asked when he answered.

"No, man. How'd it go today?"

"Interesting. Look, I need a favor. Can you set up something with Leatrice for me?" I asked.

"This have anything to do with the Farrar clan?"

"Yeah," I admitted.

"Galatians five, verses nineteen through twenty-one says, '*When you follow the desires of your sinful nature, the results are very clear: sexual immorality, impurity, lustful pleasures, idolatry, sorcery, hostility, quarreling, jealousy, outbursts of anger, selfish ambition, dissension, division, envy, drunkenness, wild parties, and other sins like these. Let me tell you again, as I have before, that anyone living that sort of life will not inherit the Kingdom of God.*'" Silence followed.

"You emphasize sorcery on purpose, Tay?"

"I just don't know if I want Leatrice being dragged into anything like this."

"Just today you told me you got my back," I said.

"And I do. I do, man. But you're not asking for my help. This is about Leatrice. You need me, I'm there for you, brother. But Leatrice, she's my lady."

"I promise not to get her involved in anything, all right? I just need one thing, one favor," I pressed.

"Yeah? What's that?"

I shared with him what was on my mind.

CHAPTER FIFTEEN

I felt too wound up to sleep. I tossed, I turned, I fluffed up my pillow, but nothing worked. Finally, I reached over to the nightstand and switched on the lamp. The digital clock showed 11:42 in bold, red numbers. Staying up might seem like my only option, but I'd pay for it in a few hours when that annoying buzzer sounded, announcing that it was time to get up and stay up for the day.

I cupped my hands and scrubbed my face with my palms and looked around my room. It was pretty dull, but I preferred it that way. Nothing hung on the walls. My furniture was cheap and looked it, but it served its purpose. The dresser top was the most cluttered. A silver tray on top held my wallet, watch, change, cross, and gold chain. Behind it was a short row of books on Christian living. I kept it simple. I was done with flashy. I ran my fingers through my hair before picking up my Bible.

I own four Bibles. I keep a big, fat study Bible snug in a Bible cover, complete with zippered pockets where I store a notebook, pens, pencils, and a highlighter. I take that one to church each week. In my car I have a small pocket Bible. It fits easily into the pocket of my jeans, front or back. In my closet is a brand-new, extra-large print, ultra-thin Bible. I can read verses out of it from a mile away. It had been on sale for such a good price that I wasn't able to pass it up. Sure, my eyesight is fine now, but in ten years, who can say for sure?

The one I keep on the nightstand is my favorite Bible. It was given to me as a sort of gift. It is bound in genuine black leather. The gold edges of the paper are indexed with thumb tabs to make it easier to find particular books more quickly. It isn't the quality of the Bible that makes it special. It could be tattered and torn—although it was clearly well used before it was passed into my hands as a gift—but it would still be the Bible I cherish the most.

I opened the cover and removed a photograph of Nicholas and me, our arms wrapped around each other's shoulders. Both of us were smiling. Nicholas had given me the Bible. Nicholas—my kid brother. Using a black flair pen, he had written a quote from D. L. Moody:

**This book will keep me from sin,
or sin will keep me from this book.**

The mol|Ech Prophecy

I closed the Bible and studied the picture as I'd done innumerable times before. Each time I expected to see something new in the picture, something different. In truth, if I'd been born with even an ounce of artistic ability, I'd be able to duplicate the photograph on canvas from memory alone and not leave out one detail.

Nicholas and I wore New York Yankees ball caps. During this time, instead of wearing his pale blue hospital gown, he wore a Yankees jersey. Every time we watched a game together in his room, he'd pull on his jersey and ball cap. I'd given those to him.

The countless days and nights we spent together watching the Yankees on television while he was in the hospital should have blended into one constant blur, but they didn't. I could recall individual times, despite the repetition—each day special, each game unique, and our time together memorable.

Though the doctors allowed Nicholas to eat hotdogs, hospital food tasted too bland for any human being to enjoy. So on game days, I'd always stop out at Nick Tahou's and pick up a couple of "garbage plates," which were renowned in Rochester. This was either two hotdogs, two hamburgers, or two cheeseburgers over a healthy scoop of macaroni salad and home fries, smothered in a meat hot sauce, ketchup, mustard, and onions.

Thomas Phillips

I am not sure the doctors would have allowed a garbage plate. The nurses knew. When they saw me pretend to sneak into his room with a grease-soaked brown paper bag, they always looked the other way, a smile on their lips....

I hated hospitals. I hated the way they smelled. I hated hearing the moans coming from rooms where lonely patients suffered. Most of all I hated the thought of death. If it weren't for Nicholas being so sick, I don't think I'd ever set foot in a hospital.

Despite the nice contemporary look of the hospital on the first floor—hardwood floors, tasteful art, plaques, information center, gift shop, and general waiting area—there was no mistaking what awaited visitors on the upper levels.

As I reached the bank of elevators, I used my elbow to press the "up" button. I did not want or need the germs covering that button spread all over my finger. I didn't want to get sick, but that wasn't the point. Nicholas was susceptible. A simple cold could kill him.

Stepping off the elevator, I was immediately thankful that the hot dog plates I carried reeked of onions and hot sauce, masking the unmistakable, acrid smell of urine and disinfectant. That dank odor was absorbed into the tiled floor and every brick and beam in the place.

There was another scent I wished to avoid smelling. It was not as prominent as the urine, but it was present. The smell of sickness was so constant it was almost visible. How nurses and doctors worked in this environment amazed me. They had to sense it, the smell of sickness, as if it were a living being on each floor. Didn't they fear it? Didn't they worry that it would eventually attach itself to them, to their clothing, and follow them around? Follow them home? Rub off onto the ones they loved?

When a butcher gets home from work, the smell of blood is all over him, even after washing. A kid who works at McDonald's will always smell like French fries. Someone who works on cars will always smell like oil. Wouldn't a doctor always smell like sickness?

What keeps the doctor from getting sick?

I hated hospitals.

The lack of warmth made the main aisles depressing enough to walk, but when I rounded the corner to my brother's wing, it was like cutting open a main artery. Patient rooms lined both sides of the wing. The smells intensified. Patients sat in chairs in doorways, desperate for someone to pay attention to them. Nurse and doctor stations were double and triple manned. Buzzers sounded. Lights flashed. The staff moved at breakneck speed, in and out of rooms, to and from carts, barking out orders and rushing off in different, seemingly chaotic directions.

The insanity was nearly unbearable. As usual, I felt claustrophobic walking toward the end of the wing where my brother's room was. I protectively clung to the Tahou's bag, lowered my head, picked up my pace to an almost-run, and only slowed after entering the sanctuary of my brother's private room.

"What took you so long? You almost missed the start of the game," Nicholas said. He was thirteen. Because his hair had fallen out, his ball cap fit loosely on his small head. His ears looked mammoth sticking out on either side.

I set the bag down on the roll-away food tray, next to his Bible, and hugged him hello. "But it didn't start," I said.

"Not yet," he said.

I quickly washed my hands in the bathroom, scrubbing away any germs or sickness that might have attached itself to my flesh on the walk from the main entrance to my brother's room. "Was mom up today?" I shouted.

"She called," he said. Someone else might not

have heard the disappointment in his voice. Not me. I heard it.

Mom drank all the time. She couldn't hold down a job. It was the way she handled life. Since Nicholas had gotten sick a year before, she drank even more. I didn't care anymore; she could drink herself unconscious every night. It didn't matter to me. What bothered me was that her drunkenness kept her from coming to the hospital. She was too weak a person to be here for him. Nicholas was sick. Dying. I was his big brother. I'd be here. He liked that, but all he really wanted was his mother.

We didn't know our father. I'm not sure my mother knew our father. I suspected Nicholas and I were only half brothers. Mom never said. I never asked. It made no difference.

I had to be it all: mom and dad and big brother. Fortunately Mom's lack of employment qualified Nicholas and me for state health-care coverage. Everything else came from me. The insurance covered a semiprivate room. I paid cash to have him moved to a private room. I paid to keep his phone activated, and for his cable TV. I bought groceries and brought home booze to keep Mom's constant buzz constant. Compliments of my employment with King.

When I came out of the bathroom, Nicholas was already pulling the garbage plates out of the bag.

I helped wheel his food tray back into place. I took my Styrofoam hot dog plate and sat in the high-back chair next to his bed. Watching Nicholas out of the corner of my eye, I was surprised as always to see him smiling as he stared wide-eyed up at the television mounted to the wall just below the ceiling.

It was like he gave no thought to the machines bleeping and blipping, standing like imposing and mysterious shadows behind his bed. How could he ignore the needles plunged into his arms? The tubes dripping medication and strange stuff into his body? How could he smile knowing…what he knows about his imminent, inescapable….

"How's the food?" I asked, forcing myself to stop thinking.

He'd just shoved a forkful of everything into his mouth. Sitting Indian-style on the mattress, he bounced his head up and down enthusiastically. "Perfect," he said before he finished chewing.

"Well, thanks for that peek show," I teased, playfully putting down my plastic fork and knife. "Guess I'm done eating." I crossed my arms over my chest, pretending to be upset.

He laughed. That was all I wanted. To make him laugh.

The mo|Ech Prophecy

"Hey, Nicholas," I said out loud, staring at the photograph. I couldn't hear his laugh anymore. I remember him laughing, though I couldn't hear it in my head, not anymore. But I remember how I'd felt those last few months whenever I heard him laugh. I'd felt hopeful.

"Yankees won, huh? They beat the Orioles in Baltimore, seven-three, didn't they?"

I tucked the picture between the pages of the Bible, set the Bible down, and switched off the light. I still wasn't tired, but I didn't think I'd be able to concentrate on reading.

Lord, I prayed silently. *Where is Nancy? Is she all right? I pray You're watching over her and keeping an eye on her sister, as well.*

I smiled. There was a time when I thought prayers had to be formatted and mundane. Prayers repeated from memory. It wasn't until a few years ago that I finally came to understand that God doesn't want to hear some recited prayer. Though it took time, more than three quarters of my life, to get it, I got it. Jesus wants a relationship with us. A friendship.

I know what it's like to lose a sibling, God. I want to help Stacey find her sister. Please guide me, stay by me, and at the same time let her clearly see in me all the work that You have done. In Jesus' name, amen.

Chapter Sixteen

Tuesday evening, while I was on my way to pick up Tay at his place, my cell rang. Using hands-free, I answered. "Hello?"

"Tommy? It's Stacey."

"What's going on?" I asked, pulling into Tay's driveway. I honked the horn. Tay showed up in the front doorway and held up a finger, letting me know he'd be right out.

"I'm just checking in," she said. "You busy?"

The question sounded innocent enough. *You busy?* But I sensed a hint of skepticism. And this was exactly what I'd been looking to avoid. It was the reason why I wanted to tell her I was done looking for her sister. I didn't need to be hounded. I knew what I was doing, and I knew what needed to be done. I didn't need her checking up on me. "I'm following up on something right now," I said.

"Here we go again. You're following up on *something*. That's pretty vague. I want to be a part of this," she said. "You know that. Can't we work together on this? She's my sister."

The molEch Prophecy

"Look, we talked about this. I told you I was doing this on my own. I promised I'd call you if I needed your help. So far, don't need it," I said. I thought for sure she would have hung up. Cute or not, I didn't need the extra hassle.

Tay came out of the house, fixing the collar on his coat and pulling the front door closed.

"You still there?" I asked.

"Yeah," she said.

Great. Now I felt guilty. I hated guilt. "Can you be ready in five minutes?" I asked.

"I'm ready now," she said, and gave me directions to her house.

Tay climbed into the car. "It's really getting cold out there. I think we're going to see some heavy snow soon." He shivered, as if to illustrate just how cold he felt.

"It's been years since we've seen heavy snow in November," I said. When I was younger, you could count on snow in November, but the last several years of global warming had allowed autumn to keep winter from interfering with its three-month reign. "We've got to stop and pick up Stacey."

"You two got something going on, or what?" he teased.

"Nothing," I said. "I just feel bad for her."

I don't know if Tay was buying it. He eyed me

suspiciously for a moment before I threw the car into reverse and backed out of his driveway.

When we got to Stacey's I gripped the steering wheel tightly.

"Can you relax, man?" Tay said. "You act like you've never been around women before. You were the man once, too cool to touch."

The reputation I had prior to becoming a Christian was nothing I'd ever brag about now. I was a new man, a different person. Though I thought I'd be less insecure, I actually felt more. I didn't know how I felt about Stacey. Aside from being pretty, she was something of a pain in the neck. "It's been awhile," I admitted.

Tay nodded. He knew. I'd been concentrating hard on my walk with Christ since becoming a Christian. Not to mention that things just never worked out between women and me. I was never good at effectively communicating my feelings to women, while in my head my brain worked out all types of deep, intelligent, and imaginary conversations. Making small talk or getting women to talk about themselves was simple. It was when they finally got around to wanting to know more about me that it all fell apart.

"What are you going to do, honk the horn?" Tay asked. "That ain't me in there. Go on up to the door."

The mo|Ech Prophecy

I swallowed a little harder and louder than expected and reluctantly let go of the steering wheel. As I climbed out of the car, she came out of her front door. I wanted to get back in the car. This seemed too obvious. I wasn't ready to be *this* obvious with my feelings.

"Get going," Tay urged.

I shut my door and walked to meet her halfway. Stuffing my hands into my pockets, I smiled. "Hey," I said.

She smiled back. "Hey," she said. "Is that Tay?"

"Yeah. Yep. That's him," I said.

We stood there for an awkward moment. I wanted to say something, anything, but nothing came to mind. In fact, my mind had shut down altogether. I did notice the way she studied me, though. Her eyes were so bright, as if glowing. Her smile was wide and contagious. I smiled back.

She chewed on a corner of her lower lip. "So what have you got? What have you found out? Should we get going? It's pretty cold out." She shivered as she rushed past me and strode toward the car, her hands stuffed into her coat pockets.

Other than using me to find her sister, I didn't think Stacey was interested in me the same way I might have been in her. *Maybe it's better this way*, I thought. "I think we're going to get some heavy snow." I had no idea why I said that.

"What?" she asked, sounding annoyed.

I shrugged. "I don't know. It's what I heard."

Tay got out of the car.

"I'm Tay. Ayenta Brown, actually. But everyone calls me Tay." They shook hands. "Please, sit up front," Tay said. From the backseat, Tay grinned and raised his eyebrows as he nodded his head.

I didn't need Tay to tell me I was right, that Stacey was pretty, but I trusted his opinion and, regardless, his approval did matter to me. I almost laughed. A moment earlier I had thought it would be better to just leave this Stacey thing alone. Now I was concerned about Tay's reaction.

"So where are we going, exactly?" she asked once we were all in the car.

"We're going to see my girlfriend, Leatrice," Tay announced from the backseat.

"What's this? A double date?" Stacey said. She laughed. It wasn't a cute laugh, like she might have thought it was a good idea. It was the kind of sarcastic blast that had *in your dreams* written all over it.

Though Tay and I laughed together, I may have laughed a bit too loud, a bit too long. I wanted her to think I couldn't care less—that she'd be the lucky one, not me, if it were in fact a double date. But when I stopped abruptly, I couldn't help but feel self-consciousness.

Chapter Seventeen

Leatrice lived in a rented house on Ridge Road. The two-bedroom cape was across the street from a small plaza that housed an array of storefronts, which included an electronics shop, a grocery store, a hardware store, and a bookstore. There were also a few clothing and shoe stores, as well as a McDonald's.

While we huddled close together for warmth on Leatrice's front step, Tay rang the bell.

Kali opened the door. She looked completely different when not wearing her waitress uniform. She wore gold-rimmed glasses, and her long, straight black hair came down around her shoulders. Dressed in a navy blue T-shirt, black jeans, and white ankle socks, she looked more like who she was—a teenager.

She held a textbook in one hand, her finger stuffed between pages to mark her place. "Hey Tay, Tommy," she said, showing off her rows of white teeth. She pushed open the door to let us in. "And I remember you."

"Stacey," I said. They nodded a hello to one another.

Tay gave Kali a kiss on the cheek. "Your mom home?"

"In the office," Leatrice called.

"Ears like a hawk," Kali teased.

"Heard that," Leatrice responded.

We all laughed.

With everything in the house clearly exhibiting country-style décor—gleaming hardwood floors, polished gumwood trim, matching end tables, and simple yet elegant furniture—the computer room Leatrice was in looked completely out of place.

I felt like I had stepped out of the nineteenth century and into the mid-twenty-first. The twelve-foot-square room was clearly Leatrice's pride and joy, her office away from the office, her sanctuary away from church.

She sat at a glass-top, chrome-framed desk with her fingers poised over the keyboard of a personal computer. Three towers sat tucked on a shelf underneath, green and red lights blinking in an oscillating pattern. The monitor, at least a 27-inch flat screen, hung mounted on the wall. She also had two laptops, one on each side of the keyboard. All the systems were up and running. On one of the shelves sat what looked like a three-in-one machine capable of copying, faxing, and scanning. I did not see a wire anywhere.

The last thing I noticed stood like an imposing entity at the back of the room. The entertainment center, matching the desk's glass and chrome design, housed a stereo system that would make a million-watt radio station appear inept. Huge speakers and an equalizer surrounded a bunch of other equipment whose purposes were a mystery to me.

"What a room," Stacey commented.

"Thanks," Leatrice said. "I'm Leatrice."

They shook hands as they gave each other a once-over from head to toe. I wanted to roll my eyes. Women were so different from men.

Then it was down to business. "Okay, handsome. What are we doing here, exactly?" Leatrice asked.

I replied with a brief synopsis of the last few days, starting with Pastor Ross's request to look for Stacey's sister. I ended with my work last night on the computer, reviewing the New Forest Church Web site.

"So they have a link to a members-only portion of the site," Leatrice recounted, "and you want me to bypass their log-in security feature?"

"More or less, yeah." I tried to grin. It wasn't

working. I knew what I was asking her to do was wrong.

Tay knew it, too. He was hesitant to involve Leatrice. I had begged him to, at the very least, run my idea by her. If she didn't want to do it, I'd find someone else. I didn't expect her to agree to hacking the Web site. Neither did Tay. To our surprise, she decided she'd give it a try. What we did then was pray about taking this particular path forward.

"Because they are witches, you're positive they must be hiding details about their animal and human sacrifice rituals," Leatrice teased.

"Yuck, Mom," Kali said. "That's gross."

"Maybe," I said, shrugging in response to Leatrice's question. "All I know is, the pages are password protected and I want in."

"What if it's just board-member stuff, like who's the high warlock this term, and who it was last term, and who's handling the collection of toad legs and wing of bat?" she asked.

"I just want to know," I said.

"You know the Web site's URL?" she asked.

I gave it to her. As soon as she typed in the address and hit enter, she was at the Web site. The whole site loaded in a blink. I raised my eyebrows, a bit envious at the speed of her system. "Sweet," I commented.

"Okay. Here?" she said, and she clicked on the link that prompted a username and password.

"That's it," I said.

"We're doing this?" Tay asked.

Hacking was illegal. We could easily attempt to rationalize our actions, explain them away, but there was no point. We were well aware that we were about to break the law.

"Leatrice?" I asked.

She looked at Tay and then at me, and then at her keyboard. She started typing by way of an answer. Tay, Stacey, Kali, and I stood around Leatrice. Though it didn't seem like the laptops were connected to the main PC, they must have been. As she typed, the wall-mounted monitor began zipping through images so quickly that I could not make out a single one.

Tay and I kneeled on either side of Leatirce, leaning in close to watch as she worked magic, utilizing all three computers. "What's that for?" I asked, pointing to an information box that appeared on the screen of the laptop closest to me.

"I got something like that on this one, too," Tay pointed out.

Leatrice sat back in her chair and crossed her arms. "Get up, boys," she said.

We stood.

"You know how in the movies the computer hacker types in like three words and they've broken into the other system?" she said in a very animated way, arms waving, eyes open wide, and wearing a huge smile.

"That's it? You're in?" I asked and clasped my hands together, thankful.

"No, Tommy. That's the movies." Her enthusiastic tone turned to sarcasm.

Kali snickered. I glanced over at her and grimaced.

"Now out, out. This is going to take awhile," Leatrice said.

"Out like, go and make some coffee?" Tay asked.

"No, *out* like, go home. I'll call you as soon as I have something," she clarified.

I gave Leatrice a kiss on the cheek. "I appreciate this, you know."

She eyed me suspiciously. She knew how Tay and I used to make a living. He'd told her everything. Relationships are built on honesty, he'd told me on more than one occasion. Maybe that was why, after all these years, with the exception of Tay, I remained alone. I wasn't ready for honesty, not where I had to share it with someone else. I was just getting used to sharing it with myself.

Chapter Eighteen

Tay stayed behind after Kali challenged him to a video game competition. Leatrice promised to take Tay home at a respectable hour. After saying good-bye, Stacey and I walked slowly to the car. I opened the passenger door for her.

"I like your friends," she said before getting into the car.

"Thank you," I said before closing her door.

She leaned over and unlocked my door for me. I climbed in, started the engine, and hesitated before putting it into reverse.

"What's Tay do?" she asked.

"You'll laugh," I promised. "When we were like twenty, he bought one of those scratch-off lottery tickets at a corner gas station store and won."

"Won?"

"Won big. He gets like a small fortune to live on each year for the rest of his life," I explained.

"So he's rich?"

"No. But he doesn't have to work. What's perfect

is he can dedicate himself to full-time worship ministry at his church. The church is in a pretty poor area, so they would never have been able to pay him much for his time. Now he gets to do what he loves, and the church is blessed with a worship leader who's totally devoted to the ministry," I said.

"That's pretty cool," she said.

As I drove, I concentrated on the road.

"Everything all right?" she asked. "You're pretty quiet."

I looked over at her. I didn't want to take her home. Not yet. "I don't know," I said. "It's just that—hacking into the New Forest Web site—although I prayed about it, the three of us prayed about it, I still didn't feel right about asking Leatrice to hack the Web site. Wrong is wrong. It's wrong. It's illegal."

She sat back and fastened her seatbelt. "You prayed about it? And what did God say? Did He answer you?"

"I don't know."

"See, that's where this all gets a bit confusing for me. You pray for guidance. But God doesn't talk to you directly. So how do you know what He's telling you to do?" she asked.

I closed my eyes and sighed. "There are signs, feelings you get. You can tell when God is answering you, or guiding you."

The mo|Ech Prophecy

"You can?"

"Usually, yeah," I said.

She rolled her eyes. "But this time, what? Nothing? No signs, no feelings?"

I shook my head. Maybe we'd moved forward too quickly. Maybe we should have waited for a clear sign from God on whether or not to hack the Web site. I wasn't surrendering control here. I knew it. I was doing things more on my own. And now I was dragging Tay and Leatrice along with me. I had justified the hack, and was sure Tay and Leatrice had done the same, by convincing myself that it was okay because the site we were hacking was created by warlocks and pagans.

"You dressed pretty warmly?" I asked.

"Warm enough," she said. "Why?"

"I thought I'd take you somewhere, but it's outside and it's cold out, so if you don't want to go, I understand."

"It's not that cold. Besides, I really don't have anything else to do," she said.

"It's not like some secret place. I'm sure you've been there," I said, playing it down, trying to ease my nerves. "It's just somewhere I like to go."

"Sure. Whatever."

I drove north on Lake Avenue, made a right onto Pattonwood, crossed over the Genesee River on the O'Rourke Drawbridge, made a quick right

128

on St. Paul Boulevard, and a sharp left onto Lake Shore Boulevard.

"Know where we're going?" I asked.

"The beach?" she answered reluctantly. To our left was Lake Ontario.

"Close." I drove along Lake Shore, passing the loose gravel beachfront parking lots, until we came to one of the last.

"This is Durand Beach," Stacey said as I shut off the engine. Before getting out of the car I had Stacey retrieve a flashlight from under her seat.

She walked toward the front of my car. I started toward the back. She stopped, pointing at the sound of water lapping up onto the sandy shoreline.

"Not that way," I assured her. We crossed Lake Shore.

"Where are we going, Mr. Cucinelle?"

"To visit the White Lady's Castle," I said.

She laughed. "What in the world is that?"

Once on the opposite side of the road, I stopped. "How long have you lived in Rochester?" I asked.

"Almost ten years," she said.

That explained it. "In all that time you never heard of the legend of the White Lady's Castle?"

No streetlights lit this side of the road. About twenty yards from the shoulder, using the moon and starlight, I pointed out a fifteen-foot-high grass wall and then, using the flashlight, explored the additional stone-brick wall extending up at least another fifteen feet.

"Is that a real castle?" she asked.

"Nope," I said, simply.

Playing the light on the ground I spotted the makeshift steps off to the right. "These take us to the top," I said.

"Up there?" She pointed.

I led us up the steps. At the top, Stacey seemed surprised to see that there was no castle, despite the appearance of the front. The ground was grassy, level, and only four feet shy of the top of the castle wall. We walked over to the wall and looked down. My car sat alone in the parking lot. Just over the trees, we could see the water and the moon's reflection shimmering on the rolling waves.

"So there's a legend here, huh? What's the legend?" she asked.

"It's pretty gruesome," I promised.

"I don't really care for gruesome," she said.

I thought about her statement. "How about this? A long time ago, when someone lived in this castle…."

"But I thought you said this wasn't a real castle?"

"It wasn't. I'm telling you about the legend."

"Oh. Sorry. Continue, please."

"A long time ago, a woman lived in this castle

with her daughter. They kept pretty isolated from the rest of society—that is, until the daughter became a teenager."

"Teenage girls, worst kind of people," Stacey said.

"No arguments here," I said. "So anyway, some boy starts coming around, showing a real interest in this woman's daughter. Eventually, the woman lets down her defenses and agrees to let the two go out on a date. They don't go far, just back into the woods behind us. The daughter had made a picnic lunch for them to share. And not too far away is a beautiful pond."

"Sounds romantic enough." Stacey turned away from the lake and stared toward the darkness behind them. "The woods are back there?"

I shined the light in the direction she looked. Tall trees surrounded us. The darkness was so thick that the light barely penetrated the first row of trees.

"While on the date," I continued, "the boy forgets his manners and takes advantage of the girl."

"That's gruesome," she said, suddenly serious.

"Her screams carry all the way to the castle. The boy panics because he can't quiet the screaming, so he covers her mouth with his hands, only he covers her nose, too. And just as the young girl dies, her mother shows up, wielding an ax," I said. "And you can guess what she does to the boy."

"I know what I'd do to him," she said thoughtfully. "So that's the legend?"

"That's the background," I explained. "The legend is that anytime a couple is anywhere in these woods they'd better behave. Because if they don't...."

"The lady with the ax will come for you," Stacey concluded.

"Exactly."

"So this is a place you like to come and hang out?"

"I have no idea why, but yeah, I do," I said. "I mean, just over there is the lake, and in the summertime, boats are out on the water. People are swimming. You can smell hotdogs and hamburgers and sausage cooking on grills."

"Yeah. That seems pretty nice. But right now—it's pretty cold."

"It is, isn't it? Let's get going." I started back toward the steps. "I'll crank the heat up in the car, and by this time tomorrow—we'll be toasty warm."

She laughed. "I've got to admit, Tommy. You're an interesting guy. This place, I didn't expect it from you."

The batteries in the flashlight failed. The beam of light dimmed and extinguished.

"Here," I said, and held my hand out to her. I walked us down the steps. It wasn't a romantic handhold. It was an *I won't let you tumble and break your neck* kind of handhold. "Well, I don't think we've spent enough time together for you to know what to expect from me," I said.

"You're a Bible-thumper, Tommy, idealistic and hopeful," she said.

"And that's bad?" I asked.

"It's different," she said, as we reached the bottom of the steps. She let go of my hand and stuck it into her coat pocket.

"Nice answer," I said.

"What can I say? I don't know if it's good or bad. I only know that it's different. All I really have to judge you by is what happened to my sister. She stopped living when she became a Christian," she said.

"What's that mean—*stopped living*?" I asked.

"She used to know how to have fun. We used to go to parties together. Go to the movies together. When she changed, we changed. We just weren't as close. And I know what caused us to drift apart. It was your church," she said.

My guess was that Nancy had stopped drinking, partying, and doing things she once did, not because anyone told her to stop but because once she gave her life to Christ, she no longer wanted to live her life *that* way. I didn't want to debate this. Not now.

We sat in my car with the engine running, the heat on high, and the warm, borderline-cool air pouring out from the vents. Our blood seemed to thaw and began flowing through our veins once again. I had trouble looking over at Stacey. Disappointment coated her mood, and I was the cause.

I put the car in reverse.

"Nobody's perfect," she said. "We've all got things in our past that we wish weren't there. Lord knows I've done things that leave me praying for the invention of time travel. If I could hop in some machine and zip back in time and change my past, I'd do it in a heartbeat."

I smiled as I put the car back in park. "Yeah? And what would you do differently?"

"This is supposed to be about you, you know?" she said. "But the one thing I'd change first is school. If I could go back, knowing then all that I know now, I'd study and actually do homework...."

"You didn't do well in school?" I laughed, mockingly. "I don't believe you."

"I passed and everything, I just didn't apply myself at all," she said.

"And that's your big sin, the thing you'd most like to change—your study habits?"

She leaned back in the seat, closed her eyes, and let out a long, exaggerated sigh. "I think if I had applied myself as a kid and worked harder in school, I would have avoided most of the situations I ended up getting caught in. I never would have started smoking, for one," she said.

"You smoke?"

"Quit. But that's not the point. Quitting was a nightmare. Who knows, if I'd been a straight-A student...."

"I see where you're going with this," I admitted.

"Parties, drinking, sex, drugs," she said in a melancholy tone. "I think my life could have been so much different, so much better, if I'd just have taken school more seriously."

"It makes sense," I said.

"You mean that?"

I nodded. "Yeah. I really do."

"What about you? If there was a time machine ready to take you back into the past, what would you change?"

"Remember how I told you about King and Bones?" I said.

She looked at me without blinking. "I'll never forget what you told me. Is it about them? Would you go back and not ever get involved with them?"

The mo‖Ech Prophecy

I tried to smile. "That would be asking too much, even of a time machine," I said. "But if I could—this is ridiculous."

"Please, Tommy, talk to me." She put her hand on my arm.

CHAPTER NINETEEN

It was June third. I was almost eighteen. I was shooting pool at Charlie's. Tay was on his way down. In a way, we had the night off. We planned to drink—we could do so despite being underage because we were in with King, and that carried more weight than underage drinking laws—shoot some pool and look to score with some women.

Everything changed when my cell phone rang. King was on the line. "I need a favor," he said. "Where are you at?"

"Charlie's," I said. "Tay and I are going to shoot some pool and stuff."

"Scrap the plans. Come by my place," he said.

"With Tay?"

"Alone," he ordered.

"Now?"

He hung up. He meant now.

I told the bartender to let Tay know I had to run. "Tell him I'll give him a call later," I said as I left Charlie's and climbed into my truck.

The moｌEch Prophecy

I knew where King lived, but I'd never been invited to his house before. He lived in Pittsford, owned a house just shy of something you might call a mansion. The winding driveway was as long as two football fields, end to end.

Tall pines, maples, and a giant weeping willow allowed for plenty of privacy. The house was completely hidden from the main road. I almost missed the driveway. Parking beside his luxury sedan, I shut off the engine and studied my surroundings. Slowly, cautiously, I got out of the truck and walked up to the front door. Before I could knock or ring the bell, the door was thrown open and the King came outside like a train, his lit cigar billowing a thick cloud of pungent smoke in his wake.

"We're going for a ride, Tommy. I'm driving," he said.

It felt wrong. All of it. King calling me with work didn't make sense. Bones was the foreman. He handed out the assignments. King wanting me to take a ride with him was unsettling. Most people didn't even know who the King was, and out of the blue he wanted me to meet him at his house, to go for a ride with him…and he's driving?

None of it was right. It all felt wrong.

The sky was lit brilliantly by billions of stars. The moon resembled a grin tipped on its side. The temperature was a balmy eighty-five, but the way

King was sweating you'd think it was a hundred degrees out.

"Everything cool?" I asked, getting into his car.

"We have to find Bones. I need him. We have to find him right now." King zoomed down his driveway, going from zero to fifty in seconds.

"Bones?" I said. I could have located him from Charlie's and then just got back to King with whatever I found out. King had has reasons for calling me over, for making me drive around the city with him. I wasn't paid to question the boss. Following orders is where I made my money, and a lot of it.

I pulled out my cell phone. King reached over, grabbed my wrist. "You can't tell him you're with me. See what I'm saying? You just locate him and tell him you need to see him. It's that simple. We understand each other?"

"Of course," I said. A cool sweat, not unlike what covered King, began to appear in beads on my forehead. Everything felt wrong. "Did you try calling him?"

King gave me a don't-be-a-wise-guy grin. "Call him."

Bones had no idea King was looking for him. That much was clear. So it wasn't that Bones was hiding. It wasn't that Bones was running. King wanted Bones but didn't want Bones to realize King wanted him.

The ~~mo]Ech~~ Prophecy

Going seventy miles an hour in a thirty-five zone told me that the road we were on could only lead to trouble.

Bones' cell rang. I waited, hoping he wouldn't answer.

"Hey, Tommy. What's up, man?" Bones said.

"I need your help, Bones," I said. King smiled at me. "You know where Sawyer Park in Greece is?"

"Off Long Pond?" he asked, switching from cool and playful to all business. "Near the YMCA?"

"Yeah. That's the place."

"I know it. What's going on?"

If I said I was doing a job for King, though it would have been true, it would have tipped Bones off. Like I said, Bones handed out assignments.

"I just got jumped, man. Five of 'em. I'm in a bad way, man. I need some help." I tried to sound as if I had a gut full of broken ribs and smashed-in teeth. King nodded at me approvingly as we got onto I-590 North.

"Hey, Tommy, man, I'm coming, all right? I'm on my way," Bones said, as any good friend might do.

I ended the call.

Bones and I had known each other for years now. The relationship had started as employee-boss but had grown over time. I feared for the future of our friendship, wondering what King might have in mind.

"What if he gets there before we do?" I asked.

"Don't matter," King said.

What mattered was what King had in mind for Bones. I wasn't sure I wanted to be a part of it. A small part of me wished—okay, prayed—that King only wanted Bones roughed up. The rest of me knew it was something else, had to be. King's sense of urgency was so obvious I could feel it in my bones.

Was King going to kill Bones?

Then a thought hit me like punch to the nose. I couldn't breathe. Was King going to ask me to kill Bones for him? I'd cut people, broken people's bones, and threatened to kill people before. But I'd never killed anyone, much less a friend.

We pulled into the parking lot at Sawyer Park beside Bones' vehicle. Some light filtered through the darkness to the park from the Y. For the most part, the place was dark.

"You distract him. Here," he said, handing me a gun. "You pull this to keep him still, but don't shoot him unless I say shoot him. You got me?"

"Yeah," I mumbled, eyeing the gun as I turned it over it my hands. I'd held guns before, shot them, but never carried one. This gun seemed extremely heavy, so heavy I might drop it.

The mo|Ech Prophecy

As we got out of the car, King produced a Louisville Slugger in a gloved hand. I tucked the gun into the back of my pants. It was out of sight, but not out of mind.

Bones was a shadow on the playground, slowly swinging back and forth. "Tommy? King? Man, guys, what's going on here, huh? Tommy, what gives?"

Words wouldn't come. My throat felt swollen shut. Inner heat burned inside me. I felt my cheeks cooking. A cold sweat broke out all over my body.

"Tommy?" Bones said. He stood up, the swing gently knocking into the back of his legs. Even in the surrounding darkness I saw his wide-open eyes bounce back and forth between King and me.

With a bone-dry throat, I tried to smile as King advanced on Bones. Swallowing was difficult.

"What's with the bat, King?"

Unexpectedly, Bones pulled a gun. He aimed it right at King's face. Slowly but surely, King walked forward. He used the bat like a cane, tapping the end on the grassy ground.

I didn't realize it, having moved without being aware of my actions, but I'd pulled the gun King had handed to me moments ago. With two hands, arms extended, I steadily aimed the weapon at Bones' head. "Don't," I warned.

Thomas Phillips

Bones looked away from King for just a moment; in that moment I saw the pain of betrayal clearly on his face. His hard street look melted away, making him resemble a lost and scared boy; in that moment King raised the bat and swung for the fences....

During it all I stood like a statue, watching, unable to turn away, unable to close my eyes, unable to lower the gun I had had aimed at Bones. While King beat down Bones, he accused the man of having an affair with his wife. It explained the fury, the out-of-character insanity that King exhibited.

Finally, when King's energy was spent, he dropped the bat and grunted out a short laugh. It was too dark to see for sure, but I thought the green grass looked wet and much darker in the circle around where Bones' body lay, fallen and broken.

"Help me stick this thug in the trunk," he said.

I tucked the gun away, bent, and lifted Bones under the arms. King grabbed his ankles. We took awkward steps, shuffling forward in the grass toward the car. At the trunk, King dropped Bones' legs, and with a click of his remote popped open the trunk. The interior light came on. Horrified, I saw the body of a woman already stuffed inside. She had blond hair, matted down in dried blood, her eyes forever open and staring blankly at nothing.

As King bent down to lift Bones' legs, Bones

jerked his arm up. He held a gun. He fired once, dropped it to the loose gravel lot, and sighed. King fell sideways, leaning into the trunk. The hole in his forehead was fatal.

I let go of Bones' arms. He fell lifeless at my feet.

I took the gun out of my waistband, used my shirt to wipe off any prints, and tossed it into King's trunk. The bat was still over in the grass by the swings. It didn't matter. The entire park would become a crime scene. Police techs would know King hadn't been alone. The question was if they would be able to trace anything back to me.

Taking off my T-shirt, I opened King's passenger door and wiped down anything and everything on the side where I had sat: the seatbelt, the dash, the leather, the armrest, the door handles on both the inside and outside, and the outside of the door as well. Looking to be sure no one was around and that no one was coming, I slowly backed away, walking deeper and deeper into the woods of the park, disappearing into the darkness….

Chapter Twenty

As I was taking Stacey home, my cell rang. I answered it.

"Tommy? It's Tay."

"What's up?"

"Leatrice wants to talk, hang on."

I looked at Stacey and shrugged.

"Tommy, I'm in," she said. She sounded upset.

"Leatrice? What's going on?" I said.

"They had their system rigged with a virus. I don't know. They definitely got my IP address," she said.

"What's that?" I asked.

"Like a fingerprint. They'll know I hacked their site. They'll be able to trace it back to my computer," she explained.

"And the virus?"

"I'm not sure yet what it is. I have firewalls in place, but I think it got past them," she said. "I had to unplug the computer and disconnect the other unaffected machines before rebooting the one that's infected to make sure that the virus doesn't spread."

"And rebooting worked?" I asked. I was not technically savvy. Computer people spoke in a different language, but I understood enough to know that she shut things down, disconnected everything, and was going to restart the main computer on its own. I had no idea what to say. "We're on our way," I said. "I'm sorry, Leatrice. I'm so sorry!"

"All right, I'll see you when you get here," she said.

"We'll be there in two seconds," I promised, though as I ended the call I had no idea what my presence would do to help. I wouldn't be able to help her or her computer.

It took less than ten minutes to get back to Leatrice's house. Tay was outside, arms folded across his chest, head low, like he was pouting. Stacey and I jumped out of the car.

"Tay?" I said, hesitantly. "She all right?"

He shrugged. "Working her way through the emotions, man. She's angry, then sad, then violent, you know?"

"Violent?" Stacey questioned.

"Throwing things, punching things. It's why I'm out here," he said, looking at the house door as if it led into a haunted mansion, as if one would have to be nuts to willingly step across the threshold.

"What happened?" I asked.

"I was playing a video game with Kali, you

know? And the next thing I know Leatrice is yelling, 'No, no, no!' from the other room. Only her yelling got louder and more desperate each time," Tay explained. "When I ran into the room, she was shutting things down."

"Can she fix it? Can she get rid of the virus?" I asked.

"She's like a pro at computer stuff. I'm sure she can," Tay said. "It's the IP address she seems most upset about."

"And Kali?" I asked.

"Like any good kid, she went to a friend's house." He laughed.

"I'm going in," I said.

"God bless you," Tay said.

Stacey hung back with Tay as I entered the house. "Leatrice?" I called out quietly.

"In here," she answered.

I walked into the office. Leatrice sat at the desk, tapping away at the keyboard. She turned to face me. I expected to see a tear-smudged face. Instead she looked...determined. Her brow was furrowed, her eyes dark and beady.

"Well, the good news is, I was able to hack in," Leatrice said. "Remember when I asked what you expected to find? I teased you about sacrifices and demonic cults and stuff? Well, before I was alerted to the virus, I saw an image with a stone altar, a woman's body draped over it, and a hooded creep standing over her with a jagged blade raised, as if ready to plunge."

"What do you think it means?" I asked.

"I think there may be more to the friendly church than what's conveyed on their homepage," Leatrice said.

I mentally chewed on this. I'd always just clumped witches, warlocks, Wiccans, and devil worshipers into one pot. They were all the same to me, right or wrong. "I don't know if I understand this IP address—what's that?"

"Every computer has one. Like I said, it's like a person's fingerprint. Every address is different. Their IT people will have no problem tracing that address back to me. I thought I'd be better hidden. I used the best anonymity software money could buy. Whatever software they use, it's better."

"How can I make it up to you?" It was all I could say.

"It's not your fault, Tommy. You didn't force me to do this. You asked. I agreed. If I'm going to be mad at anyone, I'm going to be mad at myself."

"I'm still sorry, Leatrice. I am. I'm sorry I pulled you into this."

Chapter Twenty-one

Since I didn't work on Wednesdays, I liked to sleep in. That morning, the building I lived in howled relentlessly, a vocal protest against the bitter November wind whipping past and pummeling its brick face. Sleeping in made even more sense on days like today.

Also, it had been a rough night. I'd barely slept more than an hour at a time. Two nights in a row I'd been plagued by insomnia that kept me from achieving any meaningful rest. All the more, the thought of just staying in bed, or watching television wrapped in a blanket on the sofa, held a certain irresistible appeal.

It seemed like the insomnia kept me from taking any pleasure in loafing. Unable to get comfortable in bed, I threw off the blankets and made my way into the bathroom, where I took forty-five minutes getting ready for the day.

As I finished dressing, someone knocked at my door. I snuck a peek through the peephole and smiled. Holding a tray with three coffees and a box of doughnuts stood Tay and Stacey.

I unlocked the door and let them in.

"You lost," Stacey said to Tay, who shook his head. "He swore we'd have to drag you out of bed."

"Normally," I said, "he'd be right." I closed and locked the door behind them. We sat around my small table in the kitchenette area.

"Nice place. Cleaner than I expected," Stacey commented.

"I shoved everything into the hall closet when you knocked," I said. "What are you guys doing here?"

"We talked a bit while you were in with Leatrice last night," Tay volunteered. "I have no idea what you're planning on doing. I have no idea what is really going on here, but I know I've always had your back in the past. I don't see why I shouldn't have it now."

We punched fists. "Thanks, man," I said. "But to be honest, I have no idea what's really going on, either."

"And that's why we're here," Stacey jumped in. "We need a plan or something. We need some direction."

It seemed like this whole investigation—if you wanted to call it something as defined as an investigation—was growing into something larger than just locating a church secretary. "This still about finding Nancy?" I asked.

"Of course," Stacey said.

Tay nodded, but his eyes revealed that there was more to it all.

"And finding out what New Forest Church is up to?" I added.

"Yeah, man," Tay said.

"A crusade of sorts?" I said.

Stacey and Tay looked at one another, then back at me.

"Who are we?" I asked. "Why do we think we should go digging into New Forest business?"

"I've been praying, all right? I've been praying since Sunday. I have the feeling that God wants us to move forward, to figure out what's going on," Tay assured me.

I looked at Stacey. She was looking at me. Tay had a *feeling*.

"All right. So what's our plan?"

Stacey opened her mouth to speak, but I held up my hand. "First things first." I opened the box and picked out a coconut-and-glaze-covered doughnut and set it on a napkin. Stacey and Tay picked out doughnuts, too. I grabbed one of the three coffees and took a sip.

"Tay," Stacey said, biting into a doughnut.

The mo|Ech Prophecy

Crumbs fell from her lip. She laughed as she tried to catch them on the edge of her finger. "Tom's told me a little about you guys, as teens, you know, growing up. I look at the person you are now, and I just wonder how you got out of it."

I looked at Tay, not sure if he appreciated my sharing our past with Stacey. I thought of Leatrice. She knew everything. Same difference, I guess.

Tay seemed good with it. "Once Tommy found God," he said, breaking his doughnut in half, "and he shared his testimony with me, getting out was easy."

"Why's that?" Stacey asked.

"I never really wanted in, in the first place."

Stacey looked at me. "So what's a testimony?"

I smiled. "I already told you. I'll share it. Not now. But soon, I promise," I said. I sipped my coffee. "Now I'm ready to get down to business."

Stacey eyed me for a moment. I think she wanted to push the issue. She must have realized that we weren't gathered to talk about me. We were focusing on finding her missing sister. "How well do you trust your pastor?" she asked.

"Pastor Ross?" I said thoughtfully. For a moment I contemplated the question. Over the years he'd become something of a distant father figure to me, which was still more than I'd ever had. I think my brother Nicholas would have felt the same way. *What is a "father figure"?* I wondered. My own father was not a part of my life, but he was more than just a father *figure*—he was my biological father. "I trust him," I said. "I have no reason not to trust him, but...."

"But?" Tay prodded.

"Like we've said, Tay, why did he come to me with this?"

"Because he knows who you were."

"Does he know everything?" Stacey asked.

"Not everything," I said. "But enough. Does that make him asking me to look for Nancy right or wrong?"

"See, I'm still not sold on why he wants Nancy found," Tay said. "No offense, Stacey."

"None taken," Stacey said. "In fact, I find it a little weird, too. I know something was bothering my sister. We didn't talk all that often, but before she vanished I could hear it in her voice—something was wrong, something was upsetting her."

"So what do you guys think? I should go have another talk with Pastor Ross?"

"It couldn't hurt," Tay said. "Maybe you could tell him you wanted to bring him up to speed on some things, and then at the same time try to get some more information out of him."

"It's a good idea," I said. "What else?"

"What have you got on the calendar for tonight?" Stacey asked.

"Not sure, why?"

"I went on the New Forest Web site from home last night, and it turns out they offer a class on Wednesday nights," she said.

"Getting Started the Wiccan Way," I interrupted. "I saw that, too."

"I thought we'd go," Tay said. "Check it out, you know?"

I looked at Stacey. "Not you."

"A little overprotective, aren't we?" she asked. I couldn't tell if she was teasing or not. I realized, however, that it was true. I *was* feeling a bit overprotective. "But no, I wouldn't go. I look too much like my sister. If her friend Alex is there and he spots me…."

"Then what? He might tell your sister?" I said.

"If he knows where she is," Stacey said. "And until I'm convinced that she's running away from everything and everyone, I don't want to risk any harm coming to her."

"What's that mean? You think the people at New Forest took her or something?" I asked.

"Not *took* her," Stacey said, although not very convincingly. "But what if they brainwashed her? I mean, she was like you guys. 'The Bible' this, and 'the Bible' that. I can't see her just giving up on God. And I can't see her suddenly all, 'spell' this and 'evil eye' that."

I didn't know Nancy, but I couldn't imagine anyone who'd been truly touched by God ever giving up on the grace and love and hope He offers. "Yeah. I know what you're saying," I said.

"Unless we're missing something," Tay said.

"Yeah, but missing *what*?" Stacey asked.

I covered my face with my hands, ran my fingers down my face, stretching the skin on my cheeks so that it pulled my lower eyelids down, until my fingertips came to rest on my chin. "You know what we're doing?"

Silently, they looked at me.

"Ever hear of jumping the gun?" I said. "That's what we're doing."

"What are you talking about?" Tay asked.

"Us. New Forest. We're getting ready to go out on this witch hunt, but do we know why?" I asked.

"We're looking for my sister," Stacey shot back.

"Bingo. We're looking for your sister. Other than the fact that she's friends with someone at New Forest—"

"The high priest's son," Tay pointed out.

"Okay. Gerald's son. But so what? All that means is that this Alex kid might know where she is. And really, that's all," I said, dropping my hands to the table. "We're letting our minds—our imaginations—run wild. We're seeing pagans and Wicca and we're freaking out over it all."

Stacey and Tay lowered their eyes.

"It's my fault. I got carried away. I let the way I handled things in the past affect the way I'm handling this now," I explained. "New Forest is different from anything I've ever known, I'm not arguing with anyone there. But it doesn't mean Nancy's in danger if she's with them; in fact, we really don't have much evidence to suggest she even has anything to do with New Forest other than her friendship with Alex Farrar."

"What about the damage done to your church—obviously done by warlocks?" Tay said. "Don't you think it's a little too coincidental? Nancy takes off. The church is vandalized. Your pastor asks you to help find Nancy. I mean, reporters even interviewed Gerald Farrar for his comments about the graffiti. I see too many things tied together not to think they're linked."

"And they might be." I stood up. "You know what I'm going to do? I'm just going to call this kid, like I should have done right at the beginning."

Chapter Twenty-two

Alex Farrar's phone number was scratched on a pad of paper by my computer. I sat in front of the terminal and lifted the cordless phone off its charger. Tay and Stacey moved with their coffee from the kitchenette area into the living room, all the while watching as I dialed.

Someone answered on the second ring.

"Hello? I'm looking for Alex, please," I said. I tried to sound friendly, but not telemarketer-friendly. Using the ball of my right foot, I bounced my leg up and down.

"And who's this?" The male voice was calm, but suspicious. Or was that me again, making something out of nothing?

"Is this Alex?"

He must have disconnected the call.

I dialed again. "Hello? Alex?"

"Who is this?"

"My name's Tom," I said. "I'm looking for Alex Farrar."

"And why are you looking for Alex, Tom? Does he know you?" the man asked.

"Know me? No. He doesn't know me," I said, pretty sure I was talking to Alex. I hated getting calls from people I didn't know. He wasn't treating me any differently than I might treat some stranger who called looking for me. "But we both know some of the same people."

"You do, huh?"

"We do. Nancy Callahan," I said. Why not put it out there? Why not see what happened next? When I looked over at Tay and Stacey, they were both frozen in a cringe. "You do know her, don't you?"

"I couldn't tell you who Alex does and does not know," he said, not taking the bait. "And what's your last name, Tom?"

"This relationship is all take and no give," I said, a little frustrated with the way things were going. "*Who* am I speaking to?"

"Alex Farrar," he said after a long moment of silence. He must have been weighing out his options. "How'd you get my cell number? From Nancy?"

"See, that's the thing," I said. "I haven't heard from Nancy in a few weeks. How about you?"

"What was your last name?" he asked, ever persistent.

"Cucinelle," I admitted.

"How do you know Nancy?"

"Church," I said, not wanting to lie and seeing no reason to at this point. "When's the last time you saw her?"

"What made you think to call me?" he asked.

"There it is again, all take, no give," I said. Tay was now chewing on his lower lip, staring at me without blinking. Stacey held her coffee cup in both hands, leaning forward as if watching an action-packed movie, hanging on every line of dialogue. What a captive audience.

"I haven't seen her in awhile either," he said.

"In the last two weeks?" I probed.

"I really couldn't say. Might have been more like three or four weeks. Have you contacted the police?"

"Actually, yes," I said. Though the police did not consider her missing, they had in fact been contacted.

"If I hear from her, do you have a number where I can reach you?" He sounded so suddenly concerned that it caught me off guard. I gave him my cell number. He added, "Promise me if you hear from her, you'll contact me as well. Now you've got me worried."

The worry in his tone of voice sounded a little forced, a bit artificial. "Oh, of course," I said.

The moJEch Prophecy

"You know what? I really have to go. Band practice," Alex said.

"I play guitar," I volunteered. "You guys ever play out?"

"As a matter of fact, we're playing out tonight. Quarter Slots, down in Charlotte," he said. "Show starts at ten. You ought to check us out."

"Band got a name?"

"Immaculate Mary," he said, and hung up.

I set the cordless back on the charger.

"So? What's going on?" Tay asked.

Stacey looked like she might begin to cry. Her eyes were moist. Her lips trembled slightly.

"He's lying," I said. "He's either in contact with or has been in contact with Nancy since she took off."

"What's this about you playing guitar?" Tay asked.

"We're not going to a Wiccan orientation class tonight," I said.

"Oh, no?" Tay said.

"No. We're going to a club to check out Alex's band."

CHAPTER TWENTY-THREE

Aside from an ice cream place, Quarter Slots was the northernmost building at the end of Lake Avenue. Beyond was Charlotte beach. Just east ran the Genesee River and a pier that stretched out over Lake Ontario. Cobblestone walks and old-fashioned streetlights lit the area, despite the fact that the water was so polluted with E coli bacteria and other junk that in the summer, people were rarely allowed to go swimming.

Tay and I parked in the lot by the ice cream place. It had taken a miracle from God to convince Stacey to stay home. Eventually she had agreed, but not without putting up one heck of a fight. We walked toward Quarter Slots. A large group of people hung around outside the place, every one of them smoking. Hanging on a blackened glass window was a poster advertising Immaculate Mary's booking. Alex stood front and center. Three other guys stood around him. They all looked angry at the world, wearing tight jeans and snarls.

The mo‖Ech Prophecy

Tay tapped the poster, as if to make sure I saw it as we made our way through the cloud of smoke and into the bar. The place was dimly lit. The most prominent feature was the sound system. The music was so loud that I could feel the bass vibrating inside my chest. It boom-boom-boomed so loudly that it supplemented beats in between the natural rhythm of my heartbeat.

Overall, the place wasn't much different from Charlie's on Genesee Street. When I looked over at Tay after paying the cover, I thought by the way he was nodding his head that he might be thinking the same thing.

Everything was wood—the floors, the tables, the chairs, the bar—and none of it shined from polyurethane; it all looked worn and weathered. Video games sat in one corner, chirping; a dartboard and a small pool table were in another.

There was an open area, what you might call a dance floor, but in all the times I'd been to Quarter Slots in the past, the floor was either transformed into a mosh pit, where people "danced" by slamming themselves into one another, or it was just where everyone crowded in close to hear the band play on stage.

The club was packed full. The bar was two rows of people thick. At least seventy people or so were gathered on the dance floor. People eyed us as we made our way toward what I saw as the only empty table around. Tay and I wore jeans, sneakers, and leather coats, so we weren't dressed too differently from those around us. For some reason it seemed obvious to them all that we didn't belong. The crowd of at least a hundred and fifty was comprised mostly of people in their twenties and thirties.

"Maybe we should get a drink?" Tay suggested.

"We don't drink," I reminded him.

"Cokes," he said, veering toward the bar as I secured the table for us, sitting so I faced the stage.

Just as Tay returned with the sodas, the lights went from dim to out. The place came alive with screams, whistles, and monster-like roars. Strobe lights came on and pulsed. People moved about as if in a flowing stream of still photographs—in mechanical, almost abstract patterns. A siren started quietly and got steadily louder until it was one long, high-pitched scream.

In the midst of the orchestrated chaos, Immaculate Mary appeared, running onto the postage-stamp-sized stage, where they picked up their instruments. Alex gave a nod, the siren was abruptly silenced, the drummer gave a three-count using his sticks, and the band came alive.

The ~~molEch~~ Prophecy

Heavy distortion came from the two guitarists, playing nothing but power chords, while the drummer, who resembled Animal from the Muppets, beat away like mad on his skins. The bass player stood humbly in front of a small stack of amplifiers, nodding to a beat that perhaps only he could hear. I worried the lyrics would be filthy and sacrilegious. Since I couldn't understand a word Alex sang, I didn't have anything to worry about.

I liked the siren better.

An hour later, with my hearing impaired and my soul feeling violated, the band ended their first set. The house lights came back on, though only as dimly as before. It still seemed much brighter.

"We go approach him?" Tay asked.

"See if I can make eye contact with him," I said as the band came out to mingle with the crowd, with the fans. As Alex made his way toward the bar, I held out my hand and pointed at him, almost like a wave. At first I think he mistook me for a fan and nodded back as if in appreciation of my acknowledgement. But the way Tay and I stared at him, I think he realized we weren't here for the show. He held up a finger to let us know he'd be over for a visit.

Tay shrugged. "So what now?"

"We talk. We're all musicians, right?" I smiled. Tay didn't comment on my ability, or lack thereof.

"This way you can tell me what you think. He's either lying about what he knows or he isn't. I think he's lying."

"I trust your instincts," Tay said.

A few minutes later, Alex sat down at our table. Two young women dressed in provocative clothing and heavily applied makeup stood behind him, touched his shoulders, his chest, giggled like teenagers. They might have been teenagers. They looked younger than twenty. They were both very pretty, but one had the brightest blue eyes I had ever seen. They were quite captivating.

"You Tom?" he asked. "What is it, Tom Cucinelle? Italian?" His eyes were glassy, dilated. He was drunk, stoned, or both. I smelled weed. It came off his clothing like cologne.

He'd pronounced my last name wrong. It didn't matter. Most people did. I just nodded. "This is my friend, Tay."

We all shook hands. "Like the set?"

"Not so much," Tay said.

"You play?" It sounded like a challenge, saying, *If you don't play, then keep your mouth shut because you have no idea what you're talking about.*

"I do," Tay said.

"So what was wrong with it?" He snorted out a grunt. It was just short of a laugh. Though it sounded like a sincere question, Alex seemed slightly annoyed by Tay's candor.

"Your guitar playing is too loud and full of distortion. I can't tell if you're playing actual chords or not," Tay said. "It's not clean. My guess is you're not that good, so you hide your lack of ability behind foot pedals and volume."

Alex stared at Tay for a full minute. His head bobbed up and down. Then he did let out a little laugh and turned his attention to me. "You play, too, Tom, right?" he asked. "What'd you think?"

"A bit over the top for me," I said.

He stood up. "So why you here?"

"We're looking for Nancy," I reminded him.

"Right. Right. You know her from church. And you're sure she knows you?" he asked.

I caught Tay's eye. Nancy did not know me. His question was odd. "That's right," I lied. "We go way back."

"That's interesting. Very interesting. But like I told you on the phone, I haven't heard from her in months," Alex said.

"Actually, you said on the phone it had been weeks, maybe a month," I corrected him.

"Month. *Months*. Not much difference, really. I haven't heard from her in a long time. I got your number though. If I hear from her, you'll be the first one I call." He pushed in his chair. "You going to stick around for the second set?"

"Doubt it," Tay said.

"What if I call you up on stage, you can show me what you've got?" No denying the challenge this time.

Tay smiled. "Some other time."

"I see. You can talk the talk, but that's about it."

"Some other time, I promise." Tay stood up. I stood up. We all shook hands again.

"Have a great second set," I said.

"Right, right," Alex said. The girls wrapped their arms around his; they stood so close they reminded me of snakes climbing a tree, slithering up him, around him.

CHAPTER TWENTY-FOUR

It was almost midnight when we left Quarter Slots and climbed back into my car. We took the parkway toward home.

"He knows something," I said. "Remember when he asked if Nancy would know who I was?"

"It's because he talked to her sometime today," Tay said.

"And gave her my name."

"And she said, 'Tommy Cunc-a-who?' So now he's being evasive. Or protective."

"Right. But at least we know someone knows where Nancy is," I said.

"Or at least knows how to reach her," Tay corrected.

"Right. And we know something else."

"That more than likely she's just fine."

"Exactly."

"Unless she's bound and locked in the New Forest Church dungeons," Tay said with a straight face.

We both laughed.

His cell rang. He pulled it from his pocket, still laughing. "My goodness, I got seven missed calls, all from Leatrice. She knew where I'd be," he said, opening the phone. "Hello? Kali? Kali, slow down. Honey, hang on. Slow down. Okay. We'll be right there to pick you up. We're on our way."

"What's up?" I asked.

"The police arrested Leatrice," he said. "A few hours ago."

"What for?"

"She was pulled over on her way back from McDonald's. Police searched the car and found a bag of cocaine," he said. "Kali's home. She's scared. We've got to pick her up and see if we can get Leatrice out on bail or something."

"Cocaine? Tay, that doesn't make sense."

"It had to be a plant," Tay said. "She doesn't do that stuff. A bag of cocaine, come on, be real!"

Tay wasn't talking to me. He was thinking out loud.

"Man, Tay, I'm sorry about this," I said.

"You're sorry? What for?" he said. "Oh, you don't think...this doesn't have anything to do with New Forest?"

"I don't know, I have no idea. It just seems too coincidental not to be connected."

"Cocaine, though? I mean, she just hacked their

system yesterday—how would they get the drugs in her car that quickly? How could the police know to pull her over? You think they did this—that Alex had something to do with this?" Tay asked, throwing open his car door.

I grabbed his arm. "We have to pick Kali up. Save this for another time," I said.

I drove as fast as I could to Leatrice's. Kali stood outside, arms crossed, bouncing on her feet to keep warm. Before I pulled all the way into the driveway, she was already running for the car. I stopped half in, half out of the road. She climbed in. Tears looked frozen on her cheeks.

"You okay, Kali?" Tay asked.

We had to head back toward northern Greece since the precinct was located on Island Cottage Road. I hopped onto I-390 North. Tay continually talked to Kali in a soothing voice, calming her down considerably.

I kept quiet.

Though clearly marked, an unpaved road led us down twists and turns to the precinct. We parked, taking in the overall size of the place. Woods surrounded the area. A big sign announced the way to the shooting range. We entered the precinct. The waiting area was tiny. There was a park bench against one wall, three folding chairs against the other, and straight ahead sat an officer behind a glass-divided counter.

"Can I help you?" the officer asked.

"We're here to bail out Leatrice Simpson," Tay said.

I took Kali's hand and led her to the bench. She refused to sit. She laid her head against my chest. I wrapped an arm around her. "It'll be okay," I whispered. "We'll get this worked out."

"Bail has not been set, sir," the officer said.

"So what do we need to do to get her out of here tonight?" Tay asked.

"There's nothing you can do, sir. It's midnight. In the morning there will be a bail hearing at the courthouse. Bring your checkbook," the officer said.

At this news, Kali's body shook. She cried. New tears poured from her eyes. I hugged her as tight as I could, rocking her a little as I did so.

"Officer, there's got to be some way we can take her mother home with us tonight," Tay said. "Whatever price you want, I'll pay."

The officer looked over at Kali. His features softened. "Look, I'd love to help, but I can't let her out of here until there's been a bail hearing."

"I'll stay," I said, letting go of Kali.

Tay took hold of Kali, pulling her close to him.

The ~~moJEch~~ Prophecy

"Let Leatrice out and I'll hold her spot until the bail hearing," I said.

The officer smiled. "Very admirable, sir. But I'm afraid it doesn't work that way. We've got no reason to detain you. See the problem? You could file some crazy lawsuit against the department for false imprisonment or kidnapping, know what I mean?"

I started to protest. He held up a hand. "I'm not saying you'd do something like that. I'm just saying that your offer is noble, but it's not going to fly. Court's tomorrow at nine. Get there a little early, all right?"

We walked out of the precinct a moment later. I shuffled along feeling mentally and physically drained.

Tay and Kali hugged each other. Tay still whispered encouragingly in Kali's ear. "She'll be fine, honey. It's one night. One night. We'll get her out first thing in the morning, all right?"

My heart felt broken. I'd caused all of this to happen. I'd reacted without thinking things through. I never would have been this impulsive when I was younger. My street smarts had dulled over the years. My edge was no longer sharp. I was soft. Weak.

At the car door I dropped the keys, leaned against the hood, and cried.

Thomas Phillips

"Man, not you. Not now," Tay said. He was behind me. He lifted me up. "Not now. Not now."

I left the tears, left my runny nose, and shook my head. "Sorry. I'm sorry." I didn't have to say it. No one did. We all knew it. This was entirely my fault.

Chapter Twenty-five

The ringing of my cell woke me. I felt somewhat discombobulated before remembering I'd slept at Leatrice's. Kali was up in her room. Tay had taken the sofa. I'd gotten the love seat. My feet dangled over the armrest, sticking out of the Disney sleeping bag I'd unzipped and used as a blanket. No complaints.

"Yeah?" I said, answering the phone. It was five in the morning. I rubbed sleep out of my eyes as I sat up and pulled the sleeping bag up around my shoulders.

The ringing had woken Tay too, though he was still lying down, his eyes were wide open and staring at me.

"You know what time it is, Alex?" I said, for Tay's benefit, who now sat up clutching his own blanket.

"Did I wake you?" Alex asked.

"Actually, yeah. Don't you sleep?" I asked, figuring he wouldn't have left Quarter Slots until after two, just a few hours ago.

"I'm a morning person. I'll sleep later," he said. "Listen, I'm on my way out for breakfast. You feel like joining me?"

"Breakfast? Yeah, I could eat. Where?" I asked.

"I love Denny's breakfast. How about the one over on Ridge Road, in the same plaza as that toy store?" he said.

"Yeah, sure. I'll be there."

"I don't want to see that guy you brought to the show last night. Just you and me, all right?"

"What's this about?"

"I heard from Nancy. I thought you'd want to know," he said. "Oh, do you know a woman by the name of Leatrice Simpson?"

I swallowed but said nothing. If I said yes, he'd know we were also behind hacking into his church's network. I wasn't worried about getting into trouble with the police. I was worried about tipping our hand.

"Maybe not, hmm," Alex said, not really waiting for an answer. "I'll see you in fifteen minutes or so?"

"Sure," I said.

When I ended the call, Tay got to his feet. "What's going on?"

"Alex wants to have breakfast with me," I said. "Just me. I don't think he likes you too much."

"It's sometimes hard for me to make friends," he said. Though he was being sarcastic, his facial expression was emotionless. "But I'm going with you."

"He specifically said you couldn't come," I explained.

"He say what he wants, besides some scrambled eggs?"

"He heard from Nancy," I said matter-of-factly.

"Interesting."

"But he also mentioned Leatrice."

If I didn't have Tay's full attention before, I certainly had it now. "I'm going."

"Let me do this, Tay. I know what needs to be done. Trust me," I said.

Tay sat down on the sofa, the blanket forgotten. We sat for several minutes, silent, in the dark.

"When you got to go?" he finally asked, conceding.

"Pretty much now," I said. "I've got to call in to work. They're not going to be too happy with me. I'm not really giving them much notice. You and Kali get ready. We have court in a couple of hours."

The nice thing about a Denny's restaurant was that there were no surprises. One Denny's was just like another, regardless of what city or state you lived in. Prices might vary, but little else.

When I walked in, I saw Alex in a window booth toward the back. The hostess asked how many. "I see my friend," I said, and walked past her into the dining area.

"I ordered you coffee," he said. He looked rested. I expected to see him slouched over, eyes red, slow mannerisms. Instead, he stood up, shook my hand, and was full of smiles.

"Perfect," I said. I wanted to get right down to business. I had questions, but right now, the pacing of our meeting was up to him. After all, he'd called me. There was something he wanted to say—a message he wanted to convey. If I forced myself on him, he might clam up. I could scare him away. I had to let him work this out his way. I didn't mind, because this allowed me the time I needed to get to know him better.

A coffee carafe was on the table. I poured a full cup, adding sugar and cream. Alex sipped his coffee, watching me stir it all together.

"You don't like me," he said.

"I don't know you."

"I see it. The way you look at me." He raised a hand in the air, flagging down the waitress. "You know what you want?"

The ~~molEch~~ Prophecy

I hadn't even looked at the menu. "Sure," I said.

We ordered identical breakfasts, which made Alex appear happy.

"How'd you meet Nancy?" he asked.

He had talked to her. He'd passed along my name, and Nancy must have told him truthfully that she had no idea who I was. "I don't know Nancy," I admitted.

He leaned back in the booth. I don't think he expected the truth. I wasn't sure if my admission ruined something for him, like the fun of toying with a liar.

"I mean, I know who she is. But she wouldn't know me, I don't think," I said.

"You're right. She doesn't know you, Tom," he said. "So what's going on?"

"Just tell me this," I said. "I don't even need to know where Nancy is. I just want to know that she's all right."

"And *you* just answer *me* this: what's going on?" The smile was gone from his face. His friendly expression had turned to stone as if he'd locked eyes with Medusa. "I've known Nancy for years. I don't like the idea of a couple of weird guys snooping around, trying to track her down. I might not look like much, but I'll protect her with my life. Now who are you for real, and what's going on?"

The passion he exhibited seemed genuine. He was acting on her behalf, going to bat for a friend. How could I fault him for that? I couldn't.

So far, nothing—absolutely nothing—indicated foul play. Nancy was a grown woman who had decided to move on. She quit a job, albeit without notice, moved out of her apartment, and neglected to inform her sister. In a nutshell, that was all. That was everything.

I had to make a call. To trust Alex or not to trust Alex—that was the question.

"I go to the church where Nancy used to work, Faith Community," I said flatly. "The pastor of the church became concerned about Nancy when she stopped showing up for work. He couldn't reach her by phone. He found out she'd moved. He found it all a little odd. And I'll admit, it does seem odd."

"So he asked you, one of his church regulars, to track her down?" he asked.

"More or less," I said.

Alex settled down some. He seemed to be breathing again. His stone expression crumbled a bit. He slid up against the wall and looked out the window as he threw his feet up onto the booth seat. He lounged like that for a full minute before turning his attention back to me.

"So what are you supposed to do? Find her and

bring her back to this all-caring pastor of yours?" he asked.

"No. Not at all," I said. "I'm just supposed to find her and verify she's okay and then let him know."

"He doesn't want to know where she is?"

I shook my head. "Only that she's all right."

"So he picks you to look for her? You like a private eye or something?" he asked.

"No," I said. "I'm just good at finding things."

"And you think Nancy's trail leads to me? Why?"

"I know that the two of you are friends, good friends," I said.

"How'd you know this?" he asked.

No way I was implicating Stacey. "Just one of the things I learned," I said. "Common sense leads me to think that if anyone knows anything, it'll be one of her close friends."

"You know that I'm a pagan, that I don't believe all that Bible and God stuff that you believe?" he asked.

"It's beside the point," I said. "I'm not looking to judge anyone. I'm just looking to make sure Nancy's all right. Nothing else."

"But you don't agree with my beliefs, do you?"

"No. I don't."

"You'd love to talk to me about Jesus, wouldn't you?"

"Not at this point, no."

He laughed and sat up straight again. "Nancy used to talk to me about God and salvation. We had pretty good conversations, going back and forth."

"Had?" I said.

He looked up, confused. "What?"

"You said, 'had,' past tense."

His lips spread into a thin smile. He snickered and shook his head. "You don't get it, do you?"

I snickered, too. "Why don't you tell me?"

"Nancy's done with God. She doesn't buy into Christianity anymore."

The waitress stepped up to the table and set down our food. When she walked away, I asked, "And what does she buy into now?"

"I don't think she buys into anything right now." He cut up his scrambled eggs with the side of his fork. "I'd say she's an atheist, pure and simple."

I didn't know Nancy, but that didn't stop me from feeling a tremendous sadness for her, a deep sense of loss. "And what changed her mind about God? She must have told you."

"Oh, she did," he gloated. "But that's not for me to share with you."

We each ate for a moment, silence between us. I used the time to think. I was dying to know what he knew. Asking would only force a wedge between us. The tables had turned. He had the upper hand.

The molEch Prophecy

He knew where Nancy was. I suspected she was physically all right. I feared her soul was in danger. Did my hunt end here? Did I have enough information to take back to Pastor Ross? Although I'd be taking Alex's word and not providing firsthand knowledge...what reason would Alex have for lying to me?

Nancy's faith had soured. She was now searching for something else to worship. Was that really any of Pastor Ross's business?

"On the phone you mentioned Leatrice Simpson," I said, deciding to change the subject.

"You do know her, don't you?" he said, stuffing a forkful of food into his mouth. Before chewing, he slurped up orange juice from his straw.

"Yeah," I admitted.

"She's in some serious trouble," he said, his eyes challenging me to deny this.

"It's my fault," I admitted. I knew without a doubt that Alex or New Forest was behind her arrest. "I was trying to learn more about you. I found out, using the Internet, that you were pretty active in New Forest. I read through the Web site and asked Leatrice to hack into the password-protected part of the site."

Licking his lips instead of using a napkin, Alex once again turned to stare out the window. "My father's the head priest of New Forest," he said, almost absently.

"Yeah, I figured that out," I said.

"I talked with him this morning."

I wondered what time he talked with his father. It was only now six in the morning.

"We're pretty confident that her hacking didn't affect our networks," he said. All of a sudden he talked like a businessman, no longer the half-wit rock star wannabe. "And we're quite certain that her system now has a pretty nasty virus."

"It does. That's true."

"I understand she's in jail now, got picked up on a nasty drug possession charge," he said.

"You know a lot about my friend, don't you?"

"Those charges can disappear, Tom," he said. "Poof!"

"They can?" Either he was full of hot air, or New Forest had church members on the police force, and maybe church members in the courts.

"We just need you to promise that you won't pull another stunt like hacking into our system, Tom."

He had me. Leatrice was getting ready for a bail hearing. "It won't happen again," I said. "Promise."

He picked up his napkin and wiped his mouth.

The molEch Prophecy

He dropped the napkin onto the table. "Consider the charges dropped, Tom."

Tay and Kali would be ecstatic. "You can do that? Get the police to just let her go?"

"It was all a misunderstanding. I'm sure the police will realize their mistake. It wasn't cocaine at all—once it's tested, all they'll find is a pound of sugar. No crime in driving around with a pound of sugar, now is there?"

I pulled out my wallet and removed a twenty. "This is on me."

"You are too generous," he said. "I appreciate it. I really do."

"I have to run," I said. I shook his hand.

"Nice talking with you, Tom."

"Likewise," I said. I turned to leave, stopped, and turned back. "You've got my cell number, right? Maybe you could have Nancy give me a call. Just tell her it would make me feel better."

"You know what? I'll ask her. Choice is hers. No promises, Tom."

Chapter Twenty-six

As I pulled out of Denny's parking lot, I called Leatrice's house. Tay answered.

"They're getting the charges against Leatrice dropped," I said.

"What? They were behind this? How can they do that?"

"I don't know. I mean, Alex mentioned the cocaine actually being a bag of sugar or something," I said. "They must know people. It was a setup. I don't understand everything that's happening here."

"You don't, me either. But I don't care. Not right now. Not as long as Leatrice is going to be let go."

"I hear you."

"So what else happened? What did Alex have to say?"

"He wants us to back off. I think he's being forthright about some things and elusive about others. Right now, I can't say that I blame him. We've been pretty intrusive and forceful."

The molEch Prophecy

"We?" Tay said.

"You know what I mean," I said. "I'm going to head home, shower, and change. You want me to swing by and pick you and Kali up in a couple of hours and we'll go get Leatrice?"

"Yeah, that would be great. Kali's still sleeping, anyway," he said. "So where do we go from here?"

"I'm not sure. We'll talk more later, all right?"

"See you in a bit," Tay said, and hung up.

I got out of my car and walked into my apartment complex. I bent over and picked up the rolled newspaper before unlocking and opening the door. I tossed the paper onto the sofa as I made my way to the bathroom. I showered, shaved, and dressed.

Although I'd had a cup of coffee with Alex, my body craved more caffeine. I started a pot, retrieved the paper, and sat at the table in the kitchenette while my drug brewed.

The local section featured a front-page article on New Forest Church; the photograph accompanying the article was of the distinguished Gerald Farrar. The headline read, "Pagan Churches Sprout Up All Over Rochester."

Though a few priests were interviewed for the article, the prime subject driving the topic of up-and-coming pagans in the area was high priest Farrar. He made a number of predictions.

"You will see a 400 percent increase in church membership in the next six months," promised Gerald Farrar. "There are certain signs that will soon become evident to all that the gods we worship are the only true gods, and that together they control everything in life, death, here on earth, and throughout the vastness of eternity."

When asked what the signs might be, high priest Farrar smiled and said, "The signs will be unmistakable. Some will appear catastrophic in nature, but these things must happen. Some will appear impossible, causing many to doubt, but more will believe. Some will appear so supernatural that there will be no denying the power and ability of the gods at work. And when these things all come to be, the pagan churches, not just here in Rochester, but all over the globe, will increase to overflowing."

This was why Alex was so willing to drop the charges against Leatrice. Bad timing. His father didn't need anything embarrassing reaching the press to rival the importance and power of this story.

The mo|Ech Prophecy

I had no clue what Gerald Farrar meant by his predications, but I knew two things. First, the article alone would increase his church attendance. People who don't know Jesus spend their lives searching for something to fill a specific emptiness inside of them. We were created to worship. Unfortunately, many choose to worship something other than the One who created them.

Second, Gerald Farrar had set himself up for either success or failure. The predictions he'd made gave a six-month time frame. Though extremely vague, people would be watching to see if his predictions came true. If nothing happened in six months' time, his reputation would be tainted.

As I poured a mug of coffee, my cell phone rang. "Hello?"

"Tommy?" Stacey said. "How'd things go last night?"

I told her a little about last night, but there was too much to get into over the phone. I didn't even mention my breakfast with Alex.

"Aren't you working?" she asked.

"Called in and told them I couldn't make it, that I had something important to take care of."

"They understood?"

"No."

"You want to meet for lunch? I've got a couple

coming in this morning. I'm showing them a few houses."

"That's a good idea," I said. "Give me a call when you're free."

She was silent for a moment. "There's more?"

"We can talk at lunch."

"Is something wrong?"

"No. I swear. We'll talk at lunch," I said, and managed to end the phone call. She seemed to know me pretty well; she could read the tone of my voice pretty accurately. This surprised me.

Chapter Twenty-seven

I took Tay and Kali back to the Greece police station. After a couple of hours of red tape, Leatrice was released. Although she looked relieved to see us, she did not look happy at all. She said barely a word. She hugged Kali so tightly I feared the poor girl's ribs might puncture a lung.

In the car I explained to Leatrice that New Forest was behind her arrest, that drugs had been planted, and that the police knew to pull her over. I apologized over and over for getting her involved. She accepted my apology but reminded me that the decision to get involved had been her own.

I dropped them all off at Leatrice's house. They wanted some time together, time alone.

The afternoon sun was bright. I lowered the sun visor. An envelope dropped onto my lap. I went to put it back under the visor on the passenger side but stopped. I pulled back into Leatrice's driveway and put the car in park.

I turned the envelope over in my hands. It was

from Nancy's mailbox. I'd never gotten around to opening it. I called Stacey.

"How we looking for lunch?" I asked.

"I was about to call you. I'm done with the couple. I gave them a large listing of houses similar to what they're looking for so they can look around; if they see something they like, they can give me a call and then go take a closer look," she explained.

"Want to head over to my place? I'll make lunch?" I asked. I'd been going out a little too much lately. Living beyond my means. My paychecks were modest and didn't stretch very far. Not to mention, I wasn't sure if I still had a job. The boss wasn't too happy when I told him I wouldn't be in this morning.

"Sounds good. What are you making?"

"Tuna melts and soup?" I offered.

"Okay. I'll see you in a few."

I put the envelope in my coat pocket, backed out of Leatrice's driveway, and headed home.

By the time Stacey knocked on my door, I already had the table set, the tuna melts melting, and the soup simmering in a pot on the stove. I let her in, and we hugged hello. I hadn't expected the hug, but I wasn't entirely sure who initiated it.

When the hug ended, we both stood there awkwardly for a moment, not sure what to do with our hands.

"Smells good," she said finally.

Her words kicked me into gear. "Right this way," I said, pulling out a chair from the table.

"I have a confession," she said as she sat down. "I can't cook at all."

"Actually, I think you said that before."

"Did I?"

"You did. Not to worry. It's not so hard."

"Okay, let me be more honest here. I don't like to cook," she corrected.

"I see. I love cooking."

"So I've gathered."

I slid the melts off the frying pan, cut them diagonally, made two plates, poured potato chips around the sandwiches, and finished them off with dill pickle wedges. "Voilà!" I said in my best French accent as I put one plate in front of Stacey and the other in front of where I'd sit.

I used a ladle to fill two bowls with minestrone soup, setting those out on the table as well.

"This out of a can?" she asked.

"Bite your tongue," I said. "It's homemade."

"You just made it now?"

"Actually, I made it a week or so ago, but I make a lot and keep it frozen," I admitted.

She lifted a spoonful to her mouth, blew on it to cool it down some, and ate it. She rolled her eyes in what I'd call exaggerated ecstasy. "This is really good."

I smiled. "Good. I'm glad you like it."

"Me too," she said. "If it was awful, I'm not sure I'd know how to tell you. Maybe I'd just throw up or something. Would that be too subtle?"

"No. I think if you threw up I'd get the point," I said and laughed.

We talked about her day while we ate; but once we finished, I told her about what happened to Leatrice and my breakfast with Alex. I also told her about Alex having contact with Nancy.

"So Alex knows where she is?"

"Yeah, I'm pretty sure he does, even if he didn't say so for sure," I said.

"And what? She's so mad at the church that now she's a witch?"

"An atheist is what he said," I explained. "Not exactly the same thing."

"I don't know how I feel about that. I mean, I always try to be open-minded. To each their own, you know? But an atheist? It doesn't sit right with me," she said.

"Not with me, either."

"He didn't say what got her so upset?"

"No. He didn't." I went over to my coat.

The mo|Ech Prophecy

"Remember back when I gave you Nancy's mail, on Sunday? I held back one envelope." I took it out of my pocket, then went back and sat at the table. I set the envelope in front of Stacey.

"What's this?"

"I planned on opening it but didn't feel right doing it," I said. "It's from a doctor's office. I don't know. But I wanted to give it to you."

She didn't look happy with me. "Any more secrets?"

I took a deep breath, then exhaled. "I'm not sure if there is more I can do. It sounds like your sister is okay, and that she doesn't want to be found. It's not that I can't find her. It's that I've been stupid. I've involved people I care about. I've put them at risk. Nancy's upset about something, and it seems to me like she just wants some time alone, you know? To think things through, maybe."

"But she's my sister," Stacey protested. "You're taking Alex's word, but you didn't speak to Nancy, did you?"

"No."

"How do you know he's not lying?"

"He knew I didn't really know Nancy. The only way he could know that is if he talked to her. I didn't get the sense he was lying about being a good friend of hers. It's like you told me, the two of them are close. He was very protective," I said.

"Knowing I'm a Christian and he's not, and now Nancy might not be—he probably feels like she's coming around to his way of thinking. We—I'm more like the enemy. See what I'm saying? I'll bet she used to pray that he'd come around to her way of thinking and become a Christian."

"So that's it? You're done?"

"I'm not sure."

Stacey stood up and put on her coat. "I better get back to work. Thank you for lunch."

"Stacey," I said.

"I'm not mad. I'm not. I just have to get back to work," she said.

I didn't believe her. I wasn't going to force her to stay. I wanted her to want to stay. At the door we said one more good-bye. I didn't say I'd call her. She didn't say she'd call me.

I shut and locked the door. I plopped onto my sofa and stared at the blank television screen. This had not gone the way I'd hoped.

Letting her just drive away was not going to make things better. Going after her, telling her how I felt about her—that was the only real option. Getting up the courage to do so was another matter altogether. What if she was so upset with me that she rejected my feelings? Risking rejection did not sound like much fun. Guys in general were not good at this, and I was worse than most.

The mo|Ech Prophecy

I gained nothing by sitting here, though, letting her leave....

Decidedly, I jumped up to my feet. I rushed the door and pulled it open.

She stood there, about to knock.

"Stacey," I said. "I—"

"She's pregnant," she said. With one hand she waved a sheet of paper in my face; the other held a torn-open envelope.

"What?"

"Nancy. She's three months pregnant."

Chapter Twenty-eight

I drove fifteen miles an hour over the speed limit. Stacey sat in the passenger seat beside me. She didn't speak. Although she might not understand the thoughts spinning around in my head, she seemed to know that now was not the time to ask a lot of questions. Part of me wanted to explain everything to her, but another part of me knew I was far too upset to talk civilly. I concentrated on the road, keeping a white-knuckled grip on the steering wheel until we reached the Faith Community Church parking lot.

I flinched, looking at the black spray paint. It made the church look run-down and dirty. I wondered when and how it would be removed. The image it conveyed was ghastly.

"I want you to wait here," I said. I pulled into the front loop and got out of the car, leaving the engine running. I entered the front foyer and strode toward Pastor Ross's office.

Apparently a secretary had not yet been hired to replace Nancy. Her desk looked the same as it had on Sunday. With no first line of defense to obstruct me, I barged into Pastor Ross's office without knocking.

Pastor Ross looked startled.

Assistant Pastor Alan Reddinger spun around to look at me. He was seated in a chair in front of Ross's desk. The writing tablet and pen he'd been holding fell from his hands.

"Tommy?" Pastor Ross said.

"We need to talk," I said.

Pastor Ross tried to smile. "I'm kind of in the middle of something here," he said. "Do you mind if we wrap up?"

Reddinger leaned over and retrieved his things. He stood up. "We can finish this another time," he said.

Pastor Ross nodded.

Reddinger slowly walked past me. "Want the door open?" he asked Ross.

"Closed is fine," Ross said.

I watched as Reddinger slowly closed the door behind him.

"What is going on?" Ross asked. "Does this have to do with Nancy?"

"She's pregnant," I said. "But you knew that, didn't you?"

Ross got to his feet. "What?"

He was good all right, a genuine actor. "Don't

give me that," I said. "I knew there had to be some reason why you wanted Nancy found. Experience has taught me that you don't track someone down for nothing."

"I was concerned about her," he tried.

"You were concerned about the scandal!"

"I have no idea what you're talking about." He came around to the front of his desk. Not a good idea. I considered that confrontational. At this point, I didn't care that he was a pastor. He was a married man, a respected figure, a leader of thousands, and that's what made his actions so terribly vile. I would have no problem punching him.

"Don't come any closer," I ordered.

"I did not get Nancy pregnant," he said. "Holly and I are very, very happy together."

"You should be ashamed of yourself," I said, ignoring his pleas of innocence. "Tell me this—what were you going to do when I found her? You had to have a plan worked out. Were you going to pay her off to keep her mouth shut?"

"Tommy, I didn't know she was pregnant, I assure you. But more importantly, Nancy and I did not have that kind of relationship. We were friends, yes. But it was a professional relationship. She was my secretary. That's all."

I almost believed him. "That's not good enough, Ross." I always called him pastor. I would have

199

considered not doing so disrespectful. I felt no respect toward this man now. He'd forfeited that honor.

"Tommy, please. I have not had sex with any woman other than my wife. I have always been faithful to her. You've got to believe me," he said. "Look, I can see how this would look to you. I can. I believe I would feel the way you do if the shoe were on the other foot. It makes sense. I ask you to find my secretary who's missing. You do, but you learn that she's pregnant. But surely she couldn't have told you I was the father. There's no way she'd have told you that."

He was right. I hadn't talked to her. She hadn't told me Ross was the father. "Oh? Why not?"

"Because I never slept with her." He started to cry.

Tears would have been as good as a confession had they been shed by anyone else. I stared at Ross completely confused. Did I believe him? Why should I? I was left with only one choice. I still needed to find and talk to Nancy. I didn't just want the truth; I needed it.

As I stormed out of Ross's office, slamming the door shut behind me, I ignored Reddinger, who stood in his doorway watching and biting down on his upper lip, his body statue-still.

I made my way to the foyer and out into the cold November day.

Chapter Twenty-nine

Though it was only twenty or so yards from the church to where I'd parked, I don't remember the walk to my car. I climbed into it and punched the steering wheel. Stacey flinched.

"Sorry," I mumbled.

"What'd he say?" she asked.

"He denied it, of course."

"Being the father? Or having the affair?"

"Both."

"What'd you tell him?"

I hadn't really told him anything. "We need to find Nancy," I said.

"That's what you told him?"

"That's what I need to do," I said.

"Isn't that what we've been doing?" she asked.

"It's different. I need to hear the truth from her."

Did Nancy sneak off because she was pregnant, ashamed, feeling guilty? Was Ross responsible? If he wasn't, had he known the truth all along? Is that why he asked me to look for her?

The molEch Prophecy

It was possible that she had told him about the pregnancy and that Ross wasn't the father but was genuinely concerned. And if that had been the case, when he'd asked me to look for her, there would have been no reason for him to share any of that personal information. In fact, if he had known about the pregnancy, telling me might have been an ethical violation. I knew whatever a priest was told in a confessional was confidential—even a court of law couldn't get a priest to break such a confidence. Were pastors held to similar standards?

As I drove away from Faith, Stacey reached over and patted my leg. "This is tough for you," she said.

"What?"

"Learning that your pastor is human," she said.

It sounded like a dig against Christianity. I bit my tongue. I didn't want to get into this. Not right now. Maybe because I knew her comment, however it was meant, was true.

"No one's sinless," she continued. "You, of all people, should know that."

I felt a little lightheaded. I wanted to talk this out. Not with Stacey. She didn't understand. She wasn't a Christian. She couldn't comprehend the seriousness of this situation. I really wanted to call

Tay. He was with Leatrice. I didn't want to bother them, though.

I wished Nicholas were here.

"You're crying," she said.

"What?" I hadn't realized I'd been crying, but now I felt the tears rolling down my cheeks.

"Let's pull over somewhere," she said.

"I need to get home," I said. Her car was at my place. She could take off. I just wanted to be alone. I needed time alone. I felt betrayed. I'd put my trust in God but had been led to do so because of Pastor Ross. I took notes during his sermons. I built my Christian foundation on the Bible but used Pastor Ross's teachings to make sense of it all.

Maybe I had Pastor Ross up on a pedestal where he never should have been placed. I didn't worship the guy, but I did respect him. I trusted him. I considered him a man of God who was here to help set an example for us to follow, in addition to the example set forth by Jesus. Was that wrong of me?

At my apartment complex I parked by Stacey's car. "Look, I'll be in touch," I said, as I shut the engine and got out of my car.

"Tommy, let's talk," she tried.

"I just want to be alone for a little while. I'll call you, I promise."

"Let me come up with you. We don't have to talk right now," she said.

"I don't think so," I said, without looking at her, and made my way up the front step. The bitter cold wind whipped around me, as if trying to pass through me. I shivered as I pushed open the lobby door.

Stacey was right behind me. "I just want to be with you."

"I think you should go," I said.

"Why?"

I laughed. Nothing was funny. "What do you mean, 'Why'? Because I said I think you should go. That's why. I don't want you around right now."

"That's too bad," she said.

"I'm not playing a game here."

Too many thoughts, mixed with a host of emotions, flooded my brain. In a way I wanted to be able to open up. I just wasn't sure I knew how. I was used to being alone. I hated being alone. I wanted to be able to talk to someone about real things, about my feelings, but that took so much trust—more trust than I had for most people. I trusted Tay. I trusted Nicholas. Nicholas was gone. Tay was busy.

Stacey didn't budge. We stared at each other like kids waiting to see who'd blink first.

"Fine, come on in," I said and turned away from her. I don't know if I was being stubborn, or if I was just scared.

I unlocked my door, pushed it open. When

I looked back, Stacey was still by the front lobby door. I stood with my hands out, silently asking, *Now what?*

"You told me a little about the person you were, and as bad as it all sounded, I'm not sure you're any better of a person now." She left the lobby and hurried down the stairs toward her car.

I stood there for a few seconds. Then I felt it in my heart. "Stacey! Stacey, wait!"

I raced outside, just as she was closing her car door. I knocked on her window. "Stacey, wait!"

She lowered the window.

"Come in. I need someone I can talk to," I said.

Chapter Thirty

We sat on my sofa, holding cups of hot cocoa with tiny marshmallows floating around on top. She sat next to me, but not too close, her legs tucked up under her.

"How'd you go from thug to Bible-thumper?" she asked, starting the conversation ball rolling.

Valid question. "My brother."

"I didn't realize you had a brother."

"His name was Nicholas," I said, setting down my cocoa. It was in my throat again—the pain, the loss. I kept it down and away. I always worked to keep it down and away.

"I'm sorry," she said. She understood that I'd used the past tense when talking about Nicholas. She slid a little closer to where I sat and placed a hand on my shoulder.

"He was just a kid," I started. "A good kid, too. Not like me. He did well in school and helped our mother out around the house. He didn't get into trouble or anything." I knew I had tears pooling again, so I wiped them away. "Then, I don't know, for quite awhile he was very tired, always taking naps and stuff. Our mother was an alcoholic, so being home, being around her...it wasn't a very warm and loving environment, you know? I figured he was just depressed. The way things were going—there wasn't much to look forward to. I was running with a rough crowd, pretty much dropped out of school, and mom was passed out half the time, when she wasn't she was out at bars or talking gibberish."

I stood up and ran my hands through my hair.

"You don't have to keep going," she said.

"I want to," I said. I needed to. Tay knew most of this, but mainly because he'd been a part of my life when it all happened. I'd never really had to talk to him about it. He was there.

I sat on the floor in front of Stacey and rested my back against the sofa.

"One day," I began, but couldn't say anything else.

"It's all right," she whispered.

"One day," I said again. "It was nighttime, really. I came home and Mom's out cold on the floor, an empty bottle of Jack just a few feet from her outstretched arm, and I hear someone crying. Not sobbing, but crying. I flip on the light switch in Nicholas's room, but he's not there. He'd been in bed, though, because I can see blood all over his white sheets. So I call for him, *'Nicholas? Nicholas?'*

"And then I hear the crying again. It's coming from the bathroom. I knock lightly on the door and ask if he's all right. He opens the door and it's a mess. He's a mess."

Even with my eyes open I could see it as if Nicholas were standing in front of me. I tried closing my eyes, thinking that would force the image out of my head. It didn't work. It became even clearer.

"He was such a skinny kid, I mean scrawny. He was like twelve, but he looked younger because he was so small. And here he is in the bathroom dressed in his underwear, blood all over the place. His nose is bleeding like a running faucet. He's got a wad of toilet paper shoved up each nostril, but they are covered in blood. On the floor are all these bloodied tissues he'd used. The sink looks stained from all the blood. And he's crying, looks so scared, and he's saying, 'I can't get it to stop, Tommy. I can't get it to stop.'

"All I can think is that someone beat the heck out of him, so I'm asking him who did this to him. 'Who hurt you, Nicholas?' I'm asking him, thinking good old mom had brought home some drunk guy with a temper—it wouldn't have been the first time. But he's telling me no one hurt him. I don't believe him. I ask him, 'So where'd you get all the bruises?'"

I wasn't sure I could go on. I didn't expect to sob. I couldn't hold it in. I couldn't keep it down.

Stacey slid down next to me and took me into her arms. I buried my head in the crook of her neck.

I called 9-1-1 and requested an ambulance.

"Hold on, Nicholas. Hang on." I had him sit on the toilet. I went into the living room and picked mom up. I brought her into her bedroom and dropped her onto the bed. I closed the door behind me. I quickly straightened the living room, tossing out the empty bottle of Jack.

Leaving the front light on and the door open, I went back to sit with Nicholas. The bleeding slowed, but he was burning up. His cheeks were flushed. His arms and legs were covered in bruises.

"I don't feel well, Tommy."

"Ambulance is coming," I said.

He cried. "I don't want to go in an ambulance."

"I'm going to ride with you," I said.

"You promise?"

"There's no way they're taking you without me."

The mo|Ech Prophecy

"Are they going to hurt me?" he asked.

"They're not going to hurt you," I said.

"I don't feel good," he said.

There was a knock at the front door. "It's open!" I shouted.

I wasn't ready for the stampede. Two big guys with medical bags filled the hallway and showed up in the bathroom doorway.

I stood up.

"Don't leave me, Tommy," he said. Fear consumed his eyes. They were open wide, as if continuing his plea for me to stay by his side.

There was no way I'd fit in the bathroom with the paramedics and Nicholas. "I'll be right out here," I said. His nose had started bleeding again. I slid out into the hallway. Two policemen and a fireman stood in the living room chatting.

"Your parents home, kid?" one of the officers asked.

"My mother's working," I lied.

"Father?"

I shook my head. He knew what I meant. *What father?*

"You have a number where we can reach her?" he asked.

"I called her already. She told me to call the ambulance, said she'd meet us right at the hospital," I said.

He seemed to accept the answer, jotted it down in a notebook, and then continued with his questions, asking for my name, my brother's name, our ages, and our phone number. As I gave him answers my brother was led out of the bathroom and asked to lie down on a gurney.

"Tommy?" he called out.

Ignoring the cop, I turned to one of the paramedics. "I can ride with him?"

"Come on," he said.

I followed them out of the house. The fireman and police officers followed behind. They closed the front door as I climbed into the back of the ambulance with my brother. I realized I'd been in some tough spots before—fights where I was outnumbered, running from police, about to break someone's fingers—but I'd never felt fear like this.

While the paramedics took his blood pressure, listened to his heart through a stethoscope, and radioed in messages to the hospital, Nicholas stared at me. Unblinking. He looked ghost-white, except around his upper lip and chin. There the blood seemed to stain his skin.

Once we arrived at the hospital, he was rushed through a set of automated doors, while I was escorted to a waiting area. I sat, ignored the television and magazines, and waited. Twice I had to tell the registration desk that my mom was on her way.

The molEch Prophecy

I was able to fill out some of the forms, explaining we had health care through the state, which satisfied the urgency for information on their behalf.

What was I doing? I was a kid, only a few years older than Nicholas. My mother should be here. She shouldn't be home, passed out, missing all of this. What good would waking her have done? That is, if I'd have been able to wake her at all.

In the middle of the night they moved Nicholas up to a room. At this point, I called the house. The phone rang and rang. Voice mail kicked in. I left a basic message.

"Nicholas is real sick," I said. "We're at the hospital." I gave her the room number.

The next morning, when Nicholas was being brought a tray of bland breakfast, Mom showed up. She looked like she'd been crying. A wadded tissue was palmed in one hand, car keys in the other.

"Hey, Mom," Nicholas said. He sounded tired. The bleeding had stopped. The bruises were hidden under a baby blue gown.

She rushed to the side of the bed, hugged and kissed him. "What's going on, honey?" She looked at me. "Tommy, what is going on here? When did you get here?"

She sounded angry, the perturbed parent.

"He's sick, Mom. Like I said. We came last night, about ten."

"How did you get him here? Where did you two go last night? Why didn't you call me earlier?" She held Nicholas's hand close to her chest.

"We were home, Mom. You were home. Nicholas was in the bathroom bleeding all over the place," I said, seeing by her flinch that my words had stung.

"I saw the bathroom." She sounded like a mouse. I barely heard what she'd said.

"After I dragged you into the bedroom, I called an ambulance," I said, not letting up.

She started crying again, using that wad of tissue to dry the tears, to wipe the snot under her nose. "What did the doctors say?"

"They did tests last night, lots of tests," I explained.

"Tommy stayed with me for some of them," Nicholas said bravely. This upset Mom all the more; she knew it should have been her at Nicholas's side. Not me.

"Mrs. Cucinelle?" a doctor said, rapping his knuckles lightly on Nicholas's door while poking his head into the room. He looked like he'd been up all night. What hair he had was like a wild mess on his head. He wore glasses that looked like the lenses were finger-smudged. A two days' growth covered his face. Under a white lab coat he wore a blue dress shirt, partly tucked in.

The ~~molEch~~ Prophecy

"Yes?" Mom said, turning to face the doctor.

"Can I talk with you a minute?" he said.

I followed as she left the room with the doctor.

"Tommy," Nicholas said.

"Be right back," I said.

The doctor led us to an office. We sat opposite him in front of his desk. I ignored the degrees and certificates framed and hanging on his walls, and the gurgling aquarium in the corner.

"What's wrong with my brother?" I asked. No games. No playing around.

The doctor pursed his lips. "He's in the advanced stages of what's known as Acute Lymphocytic Leukemia."

Chapter Thirty-one

We were on the couch again, Stacey and I. We sat at either end, facing each other, a shared blanket draped over our legs. Telling her about my mom the alcoholic and my brother Nicholas's illness was not easy. However, it did feel good to get the story out, sharing it with someone who seemed to care. I saw it in her eyes. She cared.

"When that doctor said that Nicholas had leukemia, I thought *I* was going to die," I said. "I'm telling you right now I wanted to trade places with him. I wanted God to make me the one that was sick. I was the selfish one, the bad one, the one who deserved to be sick."

I expected Stacey to try to talk me out of my feelings, I think. I expected her to tell me something like *You don't mean that.* When I looked at her, I saw she understood. She was a sister. She knew what I was talking about.

"Tommy," she said tentatively. "I've got to be honest with you here, all right?"

I nodded.

"I'm not seeing how this—your brother getting so sick, your mother battling alcoholism—"

"She didn't battle alcoholism. There was no battle," I corrected. "She accepted it."

She shook her head. It didn't matter. "How did all of this bad stuff lead you to God?"

That had been her question. How did I become a Bible-thumper? I went into my bedroom and came out with the Bible Nicholas had given me. I handed it over to Stacey. She flipped through the pages. She pulled out the photo of Nicholas and me together in his hospital room and showed it to me.

"That him?" she asked.

"Yeah," I said. "He read this Bible all the time. All the time."

"When he got sick?" she asked.

I almost laughed. "No. Before he got sick," I said. "To keep himself out of trouble, Nicholas got involved with this inner-city youth group. I used to walk him there some nights, or walk him home. The place really was pretty cool. They played basketball and stuff outside, and shot pool and things like that inside, but the whole place was God-focused, you know? The people who ran this place did so on a shoestring budget, dedicating day after day to working with kids and teaching them about God.

Thomas Phillips

"At first, I used to tease Nicholas. But then I stopped because I figured no matter how bad everything always looked for our family, he had managed to find something that made him happy. Christianity worked for him, you know? So I stopped teasing," I said. I closed my eyes. I smiled. "He prayed before meals, he prayed before bed, he didn't swear. But he never pushed any of that stuff on me, except to ask if I wanted to go with him to youth group. He always invited me to youth group. And I never went.

"When we were up in the hospital he had a constant flow of friends visiting him. Kids his age, kids my age, the youth leaders. It was like a party. They brought him gifts and cards and really concentrated on keeping him in good spirits, you know? And whenever they left, any of them, whether it was one person or a group, they always joined hands and prayed. At first I didn't join in. It seemed like it was something *they* did together. I wasn't a part of them. But I always listened to the prayers. They said them out loud with eyes closed, heads bowed. They repeatedly thanked God for all of His blessings. I thought they were out of their minds. What blessings? He's dying. My brother's dying.

"And then one night, when he and I were alone, I asked him why he put any faith in a God that was killing him," I said.

The mo̶l̶E̶c̶h̶ Prophecy

"And what did he say?"

"He told me that God didn't cause him to get sick. He said that life was life. Good things happen. Bad things happen. God wants us to live our lives for Him. He wants us to give thanks in both the good times and the bad. He told me he wasn't afraid to die. I remembered when he told me this. His skin looked so pale I could see blue veins in his chin and neck, and up around his eyes.

"Before he died, he gave me his Bible," I said. "He told me that God will forgive any and every sin, no matter how big or how small. All He wants is for us to believe and accept Him. Nicholas told me that God wants me to put Jesus first in my life, and if I do that, I'll be saved. I almost laughed. *Saved*, I remember thinking. *Saved from what?* I was already in hell, as far as I was concerned. My baby brother was dying, wasting away to nothing right before my eyes; there was nothing I could do about it, and apparently nothing God could do about it, either.

"His death did not make me believe in any loving God. It did just the opposite. It confirmed my belief that there is no God, there couldn't be. I wanted to put that Bible away in a drawer, but I couldn't. I couldn't. Nicholas had left a bookmark in the Gospel of John. And after—not right away, but soon after—he was buried, I started reading from it a little each day. I wanted to find holes in the whole Jesus thing. I wanted to be able to point to flaws and contradictions, but the more I read, the more I found myself wanting to believe. First, I wanted to believe because I needed to know that if there were a heaven, Nicholas would be there, right now. Then, I needed to know if there was a heaven so that I could be there when I died—if only to see my brother again.

"It was years later that the truth of the whole thing finally hit me," I said.

"What truth?" Stacey asked, having been patient with me all this time.

"Jesus was real and I needed saving."

"And what about your mom?" she asked.

"What about her?"

"She still...is she still alive?"

I nodded. "I haven't talked to her in awhile, but yeah. She's alive." I sat forward on the sofa, rested my elbows on my knees, dropped my head as if bowing, and used my thumbs to massage my temples.

"You know where she lives?"

"I know where, but what's the point? All she did was give birth to me and Nicholas, little else." I closed my eyes.

The ~~moJEch~~ Prophecy

"You're still mad at her?"

"Mad? Are you kidding me? I've disowned her," I said. "She's nothing to me. I can't talk anymore. I just can't talk anymore."

Chapter Thirty-two

Friday morning I arrived at work extra early. I felt guilty about calling off my shift the previous day. That didn't sit well with me. People thought I was sinless because I was a Christian. That couldn't be further from the truth. The difference now was that I was blatantly aware of my sin, and prayed daily for God's help to conquer it. It was not an easy battle, but at least I was working on it.

I had a key to Phoebe's and entered through the back door, turned on the lights, started the coffee brewing, and heated up the grill. All the while I thought about the other night. Stacey had not asked a lot of questions. She'd sat and listened. The more I went over what I'd said, the more I was certain I'd scared her away. I must have sounded like a rambling idiot. My past was dark and dangerous. My brother was a holier-than-thou who had infected me with his love for Jesus. My reason for turning to God made sense to me, but would she be able to understand any of what I'd told her? If I weren't a Christian, would it make any sense to me?

The mo|Ech Prophecy

I doubt that it would. In truth, God didn't make sense at all. Why would some all-powerful Being even care what happened to us peons down here on earth, especially if He created us, regardless of whether it was in His image or not? We had to be one huge disappointment. He destroyed Sodom and Gomorrah—which resembled America for all intents and purposes—so if God was just, how long did we have before He finally got fed up with us? Years? Months? Days? Minutes?

It wasn't long before the rest of the staff arrived, and only a heartbeat before the customers poured in. Friday mornings were busy. Everyone seemed to crave a hearty breakfast before heading in to work for the last day before the start of the weekend—a bit of greased energy to give them that final *push* to maintain a productive edge for the final eight hours of the work week, I suppose.

Thinking about Stacey became harder as I was consumed with managing an onslaught of orders that demanded immediate attention. It didn't matter how busy we got, customers did not like to wait more than ten to fifteen minutes for their meals. I couldn't blame them.

As I fried up a slew of over easy eggs, flipped browning hash browns, and made sure the pancakes were light and fluffy, I thought about calling Tay after work. I hadn't heard from him since dropping him and Leatrice off the other day. If he was mad, I'd just tell him I was sorry again. I'd buy flowers for Leatrice. And for Kali. Flowers had a way of melting anger; maybe not completely, but melted anger was far better than fiery hot fury.

I slid food onto plates, set them on the counter under warming lights, and rang a bell with the end of my spatula. "Orders up," I called.

As one of the waitresses appeared to pick up an order and drop off another, I saw a woman I recognized standing in the doorway. A *girl* was more like it. I couldn't place where I knew her from; I knew the face, but it looked different. It was the eyes. So blue. Where had I seen them before?

"Tommy," the waitress said and waved an order slip in front of my face. "You with us?"

I took the slip, ignored the snide comment, and concentrated on not burning anything as I scrambled to fill more orders.

"Tommy?"

"I got the order," I said, before I looked up.

"You can't be back here."

The waitress was telling the woman—girl—I'd seen at the door that she couldn't stand behind the dining counter.

Ignoring the waitress, the girl stared at me. "You Tommy? The guy that was at Quarter Slots the other night?"

"Yeah, I was there," I said. And then it hit me. She had been one of the two girls with Alex that night, wearing too much makeup, clinging to him like he was some kind of god. Only now she wore jeans, a nice top, and less makeup—way less makeup. Her hair was not all done up. Instead it was pulled back into a ponytail. She looked even younger than she had the night at Quarter Slots. "You were with Alex?"

"Now's not the time, Tommy," the waitress said. "We're slammed."

As if the waitress were merely a figment of my imagination, the girl said, "I really need to talk to you."

"I get off around three," I said. "I get a break around eleven, if it can't wait."

"I can't wait until eleven." She looked around the restaurant, her eyes wide. Was she shaking? "I need to talk to you now."

"It's going to have to wait, sister," the waitress said. "In case you haven't noticed, we're working here."

"What's going on?" It was the owner, Dominic. Short and heavy, he seemed to have more hair on his face, knuckles, and peeking up out of the collar of his shirt than on his head. He wasn't asking a question. He was yelling. People looked over at us.

The girl did not like the unwanted attention. She seemed to be shielding herself from view, holding an arm up to block her face. She clearly did not want to be recognized.

"Never mind. I tried," she said. "This was a bad idea anyway. I've got to go."

She turned and ran out of the place, practically holding her coat up over her head.

The waitress and owner looked at me, questions written in their stares. "I've got to catch her," I said.

"Tommy," Dominic said, "you can't go after her now. We're too busy. You have to put your love life on hold, *capice?*"

"I understand, but it's not like that," I said, untying my apron. "Dominic, this is very important. She's not my girlfriend. I don't even know who she is."

"Tommy, my boy, that makes a-absolutely no sense," he said.

"I don't know who she is, Dominic, that's why I have to go after her. I'm sorry," I said, setting down the spatula.

I picked up my coat and pushed open the back door.

"Tommy, you walk a-out that door, and you a-job, it's a-history. *Capice?* You quit, you get no a-unemployment either. *Capice?*" Dominic was worked up as he entered the kitchen and began tying the apron I'd removed around his waist.

"Forgive me, Dominic. I'm sorry about the job. I promise I'll explain everything later," I said.

"You explain, fine. That will not a-get you you a-job back," he promised. With a wave of his hand I was dismissed.

I went around the side of Phoebe's and headed for the front of the building. The girl was in an economy-size car, just pulling out of her spot. I waved as I ran toward her.

She stopped and lowered her window. "Get in," she said. The window went up. I stood there for all of two seconds, considering my options. This girl was in no mood to wait. She started to pull away.

I ran around behind the car to the passenger door and pulled it open. She slowed the car but did not come to a stop. I jumped in. Before I closed the door, she managed to floor the gas pedal and the tiny vehicle bucked, tires squealing. We pulled out, cutting into traffic. A car coming up fast in our lane braked hard to avoid slamming into us. The horn blared. She ignored it, switching into the "left turn only" lane. We caught the tail end of an arrow, made the turn, and left the intersection behind.

"Okay, so where are we going?" I asked.

"I'm not sure," she said. "I might just keep driving. I don't want to stop."

She drove with both hands firmly gripping the steering wheel. She was leaning forward, apparently too tense to sit back. Although rail-thin, her stomach was almost up against the lower part of the tilted steering wheel. The radio was off. Her eyes watched the road, continually looking to the left and right. She was either a highly cautious driver, looking for something, or looking to make sure someone wasn't looking for her.

"We could do that, keep driving," I said. "But you know what? I'm going to admit something here. You're kind of freaking me out. I really have no idea who you are. I have no idea what you want, you know?"

"I'm not going to hurt you," she said, seriously.

"I wasn't afraid of that," I said, suppressing what I was certain she would consider an insulting grin. "All I know is that we both know Alex. I don't even know your name."

She stole a quick look my way, as if gauging whether to tell me her name. "Call me Dane."

"Dane?"

"It's Dana. I just like Dane better," she said.

"Dane," I agreed. "So what's going on here? What's got you so rattled?"

"New Forest Church," she said flatly. "It's not what it seems. They won't let her go. They won't. I have no idea what to do. If they knew I was talking to you—I could be in serious trouble here. It sounds crazy, I mean like something out of a sick movie. But it's not. It's happening." She laughed. She was so pale I thought I might be able to see through her. Beads of sweat covered her forehead and upper lip. She kept wiping them away with a forearm. They kept coming back. "You think you're freaked? I'm scared out of my mind!"

"Hold on. Wait a sec. They won't let who go?"

"They got your friend. That pregnant woman? They won't let her go. I tried to get them to, but they won't. They said they couldn't." As she started crying, she pulled the car over to the side of the road. We had driven all the way down Maiden Lane, made a right on Dewey, taken another quick left, and followed the road all the way to Lake Avenue. "Get out," she said.

"How'd you know how to find me? How'd you know where I worked?"

"Alex talked about you—they know all about you."

"They? Who? Who is *they*, Dane? Who are they?"

"Out. That's it. I wanted to tell you. I needed to tell someone. Now I have to get out of here," she said. Fear seemed to rise off of her like a visible aura. "Get out."

"Where is she? The church? Do they have her

at the church?" I asked. I wanted to yell, but I kept my tone of voice in check. Dane was spooked. She was already acting irrationally. Yelling would only enhance her paranoia.

"The church?" she said. She seemed puzzled by this question. She took a moment to stop forcing me out of her car as if to consider how best to answer. "No. No, she's not at the church."

She knew my car was back at Phoebe's. It didn't matter to her. She was terrified about being found out, about being seen with me.

"Is there a way I can reach you?" I asked, as I pushed open the car door and unfastened my seatbelt.

"No."

I got out of the car. "Let me give you my number," I said. "Do you have a pen?"

With the passenger door still open, she pulled away, again managing to squeal tires using only a four-cylinder engine. As she flew into a right-hand turn to head south on Lake, the passenger door closed from the centrifugal force.

New Forest had Nancy. They knew she was pregnant. They would not let her go—correction, *could* not let her go.

What the heck was going on?

The molEch Prophecy

I drove to Tay's. The heater in my car had been cranked up full blast the entire ride. After Dane had ditched me on the side of the road, the walk from Lake Avenue back to the restaurant had taken over forty minutes and left me so cold I felt completely numb. The blowing heat did nothing to help me feel my fingertips. The only reason I knew my nose was still attached to my face was because I could tell it was running.

The only thing that got me out of the car and up knocking on Tay's front door was the seriousness of the situation. I shifted my weight from one foot to the other, hoping to quicken the flow of blood throughout my body. He had to be home. He was almost always home when he wasn't at Leatrice's.

As I rang his doorbell, I called him on my cell.

"Hey," Tay said. "Where are you?"

"Out on your front step."

"I'm in the basement," he said. "I didn't hear you—music's kind of loud. Side door's open."

I pocketed the phone and ran around to the side door. I let myself in, but as I was about to jog down the steps into his basement, I smelled freshly brewed coffee. I poured us each a generous mug.

"Ah, thanks, man," he said, as I offered him the bigger of the two mugs. Headphones rested on his shoulders. His keyboard, an equalizer, and a mixer were turned on. Each had rows of red lights rolling up and down like a digital mountain landscape. "You all right?"

"You upset with me?"

"Because of the police thing?"

"Yeah, because of the police thing," I said. "You make it sound trivial. I'm devastated that I got Leatrice caught up in all of this. It's not fair to her, you, and especially not fair to Kali."

"I ain't going to argue with you," he said. He took the headphones off. "But we're cool."

"Leatrice?"

"She's all right. You didn't force her to do nothing, and she admitted to me that she got caught up in the excitement and was thrilled about the challenge. So yeah, she's cool with it all," Tay said. "And don't even worry about Kali. She loves you, you know that."

I didn't know that, but it felt good to hear it.

"So what's going on?" He looked at his watch. "Why aren't you at work?"

I told him about my visit from Dane. He sat listening, jaw slack, unblinking.

"Get out of here!" he said. "Now what do we do?"

I shook my head. "Right now? I'm not sure. I'm just not sure."

CHAPTER THIRTY-THREE

Tay and I sat around his kitchen table. We topped off our coffee. He set out some cookies by tearing open the bag and then sliding the plastic sleeves out so we could help ourselves.

"You calling Stacey?" he asked, dipping a cookie into his coffee.

"What are you, twelve?" I asked, grabbing a few cookies for myself.

"It's good this way," he said. Though he held the cookie delicately between his thumb and finger, as he lifted the coffee-soaked cookie to his mouth, it crumbled the way a sand castle does when a wave rolls over it. Most of the thing dropped back into his coffee.

Choosing not to say anything, I shook my head in mock disgust. "I'm not calling her. Not yet. It's all too weird, you know? It doesn't feel right. Even Dane, there's something about her. If I didn't see fear—I mean genuine fear throughout her body—I'd swear the meeting was staged. A complete setup."

"You don't think it was, do you?" Tay attempted to dip another cookie into his hot coffee. He didn't dunk this time. He just dipped in a rounded end.

"You thinking it was staged?" I asked.

"Sounds it." Tay stuffed the moistened cookie into his mouth.

"I saw her fear."

"Fear can be faked."

"Not like this," I said. "I think it was real."

"Could be she's on drugs," he offered.

"That's true," I said. "At the end of a high. That would scare a junkie You should have seen her. She was shaking. And had this ghost-white skin. And she was sweating."

"That sounds like drugs."

"But what about when I asked if Nancy was at the church? She was really confused by the question," I said.

"Yeah, but she said she's not at the church."

"She did. That's true. But it's the way she answered me. Tay, I'm telling you. I believe her," I said. I gave in. I dipped a cookie and ate it. "Oh, that is good."

"What are you, twelve?"

We laughed.

"Whether she's telling us the truth or not, we've got to do something," Tay said.

"You're thinking we should call the police?"

"It makes sense, don't you think? If these people really have Nancy held hostage or something, if they're keeping her against her will, that's a matter for the police."

I knew he was right. For some reason, maybe pride, I didn't want to let go of this. That was foolish. This wasn't a game, and I wasn't a teenage hoodlum anymore. Nancy was a real person, and as far as I knew, she really was pregnant. If the people at New Forest had her captive, were holding her against her will, then I needed to know enough to step aside. "You're right. We call the police."

Tay leaned back in his chair. "Okay, but here's the thing. What, exactly, do we tell them? And, we already know that New Forest has someone on the police force, right? Look what happened with Leatrice."

He was right. The situation felt hopeless. "We don't have to mention we're in the middle of some good versus evil conspiracy theory."

"You think we should keep that to ourselves?" he teased.

"Pastor Ross already used the police to try to locate Nancy," I pointed out.

"Maybe so, but we have new information," he said.

"True." I stood, walked over to the counter,

poured what was left of my coffee into the sink, and quickly rinsed out the mug. "We're still going to sound crazy."

"It's a matter for the police."

"Okay," I said. "You call them."

While we waited for a police officer to show up, Tay grabbed one of his Bibles, opened it, and read, *"Let the evil of the wicked come to an end, but establish the righteous. The One who examines the thoughts and emotions is a righteous God. My shield is with God, who saves the upright in heart. God is a righteous judge, and a God who executes justice every day."*

"Amen," I said. "Psalms?"

He nodded. "Chapter seven, nine through eleven."

Psalms was filled with verses that could be prayed when applied to life. The Bible was so old and yet so relevant.

"You know, maybe you ought to call Stacey now, fill her in?" Tay said. He was right.

I flipped open my cell phone. Tay went on silently reading Scripture as I dialed. While the phone rang, I realized that I couldn't wait for her to answer. I was anxious to talk to her. I missed her.

Her voice mail picked up. "Stacey? It's me, Tommy. I'm at Tay's house. I have a few things I need to talk to you about. They have to do with your sister. Give me a call when you get this message, okay? And hey, thanks for last night."

Tay looked up at me over his Bible, eyebrows arched inquisitively.

I closed my cell. "We talked. Or really, I talked."

"Talking's good, man. And you do so very little of it," he said.

I shook my head. "I talk all the time."

"But you don't really say anything—not real things."

"What do I say? Fake things?"

"Nah, man. But you don't talk about you."

"Life's not about me," I said.

"So true. But your feelings, man. You don't share them."

"We're guys. Guys don't do that."

"It needs to be done, though. I'm glad you got Stacey for that now."

He was right. "Yeah. Me too."

When someone knocked at the door, Tay answered. A police officer entered the house. We introduced ourselves.

Officer Dave Stratton was over six feet tall, had brush-cut brown hair, and was clean shaven. Though his face made him look eighteen years old, his eyes and the wrinkles around them revealed a much older man. Bulging muscles made his blue uniform fit too tightly. Maybe he did that on purpose—force the bad guys to think before acting irrationally. I knew that if he were here to arrest me, I'd hesitate before resisting him.

Tay invited him in and had him sit at the table. I poured Officer Stratton a cup of coffee. He thanked me while eyeing the Bible on the table.

"You guys praying or something?" he asked.

Sometimes, admitting I was a Christian wasn't the easiest thing to do. It depended on the circumstances and who was around. Being singled out made me uncomfortable. I wasn't worried about being teased. I was a lifetime away from elementary school, but I sometimes feared the whispers, the odd looks, and wondering about the unknown thoughts that ran through the minds of people once they found out I was born again.

"We're Christians," Tay said; no pause, no fear.

The cop's neutral demeanor evaporated. His lips pursed, thinning into two straight lines. "Okay, what have we got here?" All business.

I had prayed that God would send a Christian officer. It didn't look like that prayer had been answered. I feared Officer Stratton would listen to our story and immediately write most of it off as half-baked. What choice did we have? We'd called the police, and the police were here.

"Okay, Tom, do me a favor, all right?" Stratton said. "Start at the beginning. Talk slow," he said, waving his notebook in front of me. "I don't write so fast, and if I do, then when I go back and try to read it, I can't."

I tried to laugh. "Gotcha," I said.

"We might run through this a few times," Stratton said. "And I ask a lot of questions. But I ask them as I think of them. I don't wait for a break in your story."

"Okay," I said. "That's fine with me. You ready? Well, it started, for me, on Sunday morning."

I started with my arrival at church, seeing the graffiti on the front of the building, Pastor Ross approaching me after the service, our conversation in his office, and running into Stacey after visiting Nancy's apartment. I told him about how Nancy was close friends with Alex Farrar, Gerald's son over at New Forest, and how I forced Leatrice to hack into the New Forest Web site; how the police got involved in that mess, but how Alex promised not to take the matter any further; how Tay and I went to hear Alex's band, and how Dane came to visit me where I worked.

I expected the retelling to take more than an

hour, thinking Officer Stratton would have a million questions as he had promised. He did not ask one. In fact, he only took down a few notes while I spoke, and maybe some names—I couldn't see what he'd written. As I finished up, ending with our decision to call the police, Officer Stratton closed his notebook.

"Anything else?"

"No," I said. I felt embarrassed, like a kid who finally realizes he's rambling on and on and no one is listening. Besides, if there was anything else to tell, it was hidden in my subconscious.

"Okay, then," Officer Stratton said, getting to his feet.

Tay and I stood.

"What should we do?" I asked.

"Look," Officer Stratton said. His muscles flexed as he pointed a finger at me. "You and your friend here have spent too much time reading Harry Potter novels, all right. Life is not a game. When you call the police with nonsense like this, you take officers like me away from helping those who are truly in need. To be honest, I'm still considering whether or not to bring charges against you for filing a fraudulent police report. That's against the law, you know, and I have every right to arrest you, both of you, right here, right now."

"This isn't some made-up story," I said, feeling

defensive. "Every word of it is true."

Officer Stratton stared at me for a long moment. He snorted out a short laugh. "I'll put some time into looking into this, all right? But let me tell you right now: if this is a lame report, I'll be back to arrest both of you," he said, "or I can walk away now and pretend I was never here. Your choice."

"Look into it," Tay and I said at the same time.

Officer Stratton looked at Tay, then at me, and then back at Tay. "Hey, it's your freedom we're talking about here."

He left.

I closed the door and turned to face Tay. "Now what do we do?"

Tay shrugged in submission. "We tried to do the right thing. I don't think we can count on Officer Friendly there. We're on our own."

"You're still with me?" I asked.

"Until the end, man," Tay pointed out.

I didn't blame Officer Stratton for his response. If I wasn't a Christian and someone came to me with far-fetched fantasy tales about warlocks and cults, I would think the people telling me the story were crazy, too.

Chapter Thirty-four

Stacey and I had planned to meet at my place for dinner. She was anxious to hear what news I had regarding Nancy. I didn't feel comfortable talking about it on the phone, not to mention that talking to her in person gave me another chance to see her. Besides, she was busy at work and couldn't get out early.

Despite the cold, I pulled my charcoal grill out of storage and wheeled it out the back door at the apartment complex, fired it up, and cooked some thick steaks that I'd had marinating the last few days. Inside, I'd peeled and diced up potatoes. Oil was getting hot in the deep fryer. I loved home-made fries. The tossed salad was in a bowl in the fridge, covered with sliced black olives, beets, carrots, celery, chick peas, bread crumbs, and bacon bits—real bacon bits.

Though we'd only met five days ago, it felt like we'd known each other much longer, at least to me. I wasn't trying to rush things. It all just felt natural,

I suppose. The unfortunate thing was the circumstances of our meeting. I was okay living alone, or at least I'd thought I was. But now that I had met Stacey, I wasn't sure I wanted to be alone anymore. Tay was right—having someone to talk with made a difference.

I took the steaks up to my apartment, dropped the potato fries into the deep fryer, and quickly but elegantly set the table for two. I didn't drink alcohol, and though a nice bottle of red wine sounded appropriate, I settled for a chilled two-liter bottle of Diet Coke.

I kept the steaks covered and in the oven. It was six. She should have been here by now. I thought about calling her cell to see if she was on her way. I didn't want to seem impatient, obsessive, or compulsive.

Standing by the window, I watched cars pass by on the main road. I expected cars that looked like Stacey's to turn into the complex lot, but none did. Eventually, I sat on the sofa and switched on the television. And then it hit me.

I was unemployed.

I could go back, talk to Dominic in the morning, and tell him everything that had been going on. He might understand and give me my job back. Even if he didn't take me back, I at least owed him an explanation.

Thomas Phillips

At seven, I decided to call Stacey's cell phone. The steaks were drying out. I could reintroduce some of the juiciness back into the meat with the leftover marinade, but that wouldn't be the same. The phone rang five times before rolling into her voice mail. I left a message.

I set my phone down on the coffee table and paced back and forth by the window. She must be on her way. If she was anything like me, she had forgotten to give her phone a good charge and the battery had died. I hated when that happened.

Switching on the television, I sat on the sofa and channel surfed. Nothing was on. I had hundreds of channels to flip through, and none of them was worth watching. I settled on a show that showed how things were made. Today's episode was on Hostess Twinkies. I crossed my arms over my chest and watched until my eyelids grew so heavy that it didn't seem worth fighting to keep them open.

Mom and I stood on either side of Nicholas's hospital bed. His face was white, sweaty. His dry, cracked lips were colorless. Dark circles outlined his eyes. He held Mom's hand in one of his, mine in the other. The doctor assured us this was it. He had minutes left. Minutes.

The molEch Prophecy

His friends and people from his youth group waited down in a family area. He wanted to spend these last few moments with us. I wanted to be strong, needed to be strong. Nicholas wore as big a smile as his mouth would allow. Prescription drugs coursed through his veins. He was not in pain. I was. My heart was being crushed.

God had made a mistake. He'd let Nicholas get cancer. Nicholas was the good son. I deserved this. Me. I didn't go to church, didn't read the Bible. I went out wreaking havoc, beating people up, breaking fingers and skulls. God should be punishing me, not Nicholas. Nicholas had done nothing wrong; surely he hadn't committed a sin so terrible that he deserved to spend a year in a hospital, wasting away to nothing. God wasn't just, couldn't be.

God had made a mistake.

"I'm not scared, you know," he said to us, his voice barely more than a whisper.

I just nodded and smiled, knowing that if I tried to say anything at all, I'd cry. I held it in.

"I want you to do me a favor, Tommy. Please," Nicholas asked.

"Yeah," I said, managing to hold my tears back. "Anything."

"My Bible, you have it?"

The one he'd given me. "It's here," I said.

"Give it to me, please," he said, his eyes locked

on mine. I couldn't look away. I didn't want to. Through his eyes I saw all of Nicholas, my little brother. As the big brother, and because we never had a father, or much of a mother, I always felt it was my job to protect him. One job. A simple job, really, and I'd failed him.

With hands that looked like skeletons wrapped in nothing but tight skin, he flipped open the Holy Book. His eyes scanned pages as he turned them, clearly looking for something in particular. More than a thousand pages were before him, but he seemed to know right where he wanted to go. When he stopped turning pages, I saw something sparkle in his eyes. He'd found what he'd been looking for.

He lifted the Bible and attempted to hand it over to me. I took it from him.

"Read to me, please? See the big number fifteen? That's the chapter. See those little numbers all mixed in with the words? Go down to where you see the number eleven. See it? Start there, please."

Nicholas held Mom's hand in both of his as I looked at the words in front of me. We were in the book of Luke. The heading said, "The Story of the Lost Son."

"Where do I stop?" I asked, feeling a bit uncomfortable. I'd never read anything from the Bible before. I was sure it was written in such a way that I wouldn't even be able to pronounce the words, and even if I could, I wouldn't understand the story I was reading.

"Just read to the end where there is a small twenty-seven," he said. "Go on, please read."

How could I say no? As I started, I was surprised by how easy it was to read. The story was not complicated. A wealthy farmer had two sons. One didn't want to wait for his father to die before getting his share of the inheritance, so he asked for it now. The farmer divided up the estate and paid off the one son. That son took off and blew the inheritance on what sounded like, if I was reading this right, alcohol and prostitutes. Broke and in the midst of a depression, the kid found himself unemployed and scraping the bottom of the barrel.

Finally finding a job where he was treated like trash, he realized he could return home for a job where he knew the people who worked for his father were at least treated respectfully. When he finally comes home, ready to apologize for wronging God and his father, the farmer welcomes his son back from what he calls "the dead" and throws a huge celebration.

When I finished, I looked over at Nicholas, half expecting him to have passed away. But he hadn't. His eyes were open wide, and his lips were spread into a big smile.

"I love that story," he whispered. His hand

reached up and touched my face, wiping away a tear.

Mom was crying, too.

"It's pretty good," I told him.

"God wants you to go to Him," Nicholas said. "He doesn't care about what you did in the past. He just wants you to realize that you need Him. If you ask Him for forgiveness, He will forgive you and there will be a huge celebration in heaven—in your honor. It says so in the Bible."

Nicholas was comparing me to the lost son from the story. Just like God had made a mistake in letting Nicholas get sick, Nicholas was making a mistake in thinking that God would forgive me for all the things I'd done wrong. My sins were unforgivable.

Nicholas coughed, tried to smile, and coughed again.

"No, Nicky," I said. "You've got to stay with me."

He closed his eyes, then opened them slowly. "Keep reading," he said. "Promise me you'll keep reading?"

"I promise," I said.

He nodded slightly as he closed his eyes.

"Nicholas!" I shouted. I grabbed his hand in mine. "Nick!"

His eyes didn't open. Mom dropped her head

onto Nicholas's stomach, sobbing. He looked so little, so frail, so defenseless.

"No, Nick. Don't do this. You're not going anywhere. You're not!"

But he was going somewhere. He was gone. The steady beeping of whatever machines he'd been hooked up to flatlined....

CHAPTER THIRTY-FIVE

I woke with a start, pulling out of the dream I'd been having, the terrible one…the one where I stood by my brother as he passed away. It was real. It happened. Only he had not flatlined.

It was the ringing of my cell phone that I'd heard in the dream. The ringing woke me. I must have fallen asleep on the sofa. The apartment was light. I turned to look at the window. Morning. I had slept through the night.

I noticed it was a blocked caller as I answered the phone. "Hello?" I hoped it was Stacey. It wasn't.

"Did you call the police?"

"Alex?" I said. It sounded like him, but different. Perhaps he was trying to disguise his voice.

"You've got some nerve. I mean it. Nerve. You were in trouble with the law, Cucinelle. You and your friend Leatrice, there. And what did we do, huh? We worked things out. We met face-to-face, talked through our differences. Charges against your buddy's girl were dropped, right? And now you, the Christian," he said, putting a sarcastic emphasis on the word *Christian*, "you went and filed a complaint with the police. What are we supposed to think, here? What are we supposed to do?"

I listened intently to his ranting. Questions filled my head. I didn't like the fact that he was calling me. Not now. Not with the new information we'd discovered about Nancy. "You know where Nancy is, don't you?" I asked.

Where was Stacey? No. She'd missed our dinner. That was all. Nothing more.

"We're going to need to talk, Cucinelle. You and me," he said. "But the first thing I want you to do is call off the police. We've got members of our coven in the department. They told us about how you and Tay invited Officer Stratton over for coffee and proceeded to spin out a tale worthy of a mid-list author writing a *blah* horror novel."

"Where's Nancy?" I asked, as if ignoring him and his requests.

"You don't want to be sorry. I'll be in touch—once you call off the police."

My line went dead. I immediately tried calling Stacey. The phone rang and rang before again rolling over into voice mail. I ended the call and called back. Voice mail. I decided to leave another message. "It's Tommy, Stacey. Where are you? Call me.

It's important." I closed my phone and stuffed it into my pocket.

I felt a little lost. What had just happened did not make sense; at least, I couldn't make sense of it. I could understand not wanting the police looking into their business based on the complaint I'd filed, but the threatening phone call confused me. It made them look guilty.

Did they have Nancy? If they did, why hold a pregnant woman against her will?

Maybe Stacey had some more information and didn't realize it. Not that it mattered right now, as I couldn't reach Stacey. The only other person I could think to contact who might have information was Pastor Ross. I called his office.

Though I didn't have an appointment, Pastor Ross had agreed to see me on the spot, as I'd expected. Sitting in his office was Pastor Alan. He had a tablet on his crossed legs, and he held the end of a pen in his hand, spinning it between his fingers.

"I hate to barge in," I said blandly, walking into Pastor Ross's office.

"Not a problem," Pastor Ross said, trying to share a warm smile. I made him uncomfortable now, I realized. Regardless of how this all turned out, I suspected I'd be looking for another church home soon.

"Want me to come back?" Pastor Alan asked, moving to stand up, his hands planted on the arms of the chair, the pad in one hand, the pen in the other.

"Why don't you stay?" Pastor Ross said. "I have no secrets. Unless you prefer it be just the two of us?"

"Doesn't matter to me," I said.

"You know Pastor Alan," Pastor Ross said.

"I do," I said. We shook hands. I sat in the chair next to him. Pastor Ross went back around his desk and sat down.

"We're grooming Pastor Alan here to one day become the senior pastor of his own church," Pastor Ross said.

"You mean, to leave Faith?" I asked, looking at Pastor Alan.

"That's right," Pastor Ross said.

"I'd like to open a sister church somewhere in Rochester," Pastor Alan said.

"Isn't that like having too many gas stations on the same corner?" I asked.

Both pastors laughed. "It's just the opposite," Pastor Ross said. "You can never have too many churches. We are not in competition with one another. We are part of the body of Christ. The more people we reach, the better. It's that simple."

I felt my eyebrows go up. I wondered how a new church got started. Who'd attend? Would people leave Faith and Pastor Ross in order to follow Pastor Alan? There'd have to be hard feelings, regardless of whether or not more churches in a consolidated area was the answer.

"On the phone you said you had some urgent questions," Pastor Ross said. "I'm not sure what I can tell you, but I promise to answer all that I can."

On the drive over I had struggled deciding how much I'd tell Pastor Ross. Trust was a factor. I wasn't sure I trusted him. As far as I could tell, he had not been forthcoming at the time he "hired" me to track down Nancy. I realized there was no reason not to fill him in completely. I might share a piece of information that would click with him, causing him to remember something that, perhaps, he'd thought was not important, a tiny piece of something he'd overlooked.

Just as I'd done with Officer Stratton, I started at the beginning and detailed the events that had unfolded over the last few days. As I talked, I kept looking from pastor to pastor. My rendition held them riveted. They barely seemed to be breathing as they listened.

"This is unreal," Pastor Ross said, leaning back in his leather chair. He closed his eyes and clasped his hands over his face. When he sighed, it was long, loud, and muffled by his palms. As he lowered his hands he said, "I know the Farrars. This is troubling."

"Do you recall anything about Nancy—something about her past—that tied her in to witchcraft or paganism?" I asked, wanting to remind him that he used his knowledge of my past to recruit me in the hunt for his missing secretary.

Pastor Ross stood up, stuffed his hands into his pant pockets, and turned his back to me as he stared out the window. He knew something. I must be making him uncomfortable with my questions. When he asked me to find Nancy, I don't think he expected the task to become so complex.

"Pastor Ross?" I prodded. Pastor Alan, I noticed, stared hard at Pastor Ross's back.

Ross turned. "She was into Wicca when she started coming to Faith," he said. "That was about ten years ago. She was in her late teens or early twenties, I can't recall. When I thought of people at that age being involved with that kind of religion, I used to picture them wearing black clothing and black makeup, but not Nancy. Our church was a lot smaller back then, with maybe a couple hundred people attending regularly.

Thomas Phillips

"After the service one Sunday morning, as I was standing in the foyer greeting people as they left, she stopped and told me that she didn't buy all the Christian stuff I talked about, and that she was a witch. She wore a long dress and blouse, her hair was done, and she had just a touch of makeup on. At first I thought she was kidding. Like I said, she didn't look the way I pictured witches looking. Something in her eyes, though, told me she was serious. So I simply thanked her for coming and invited her back the following Sunday. I think I told her what the message would be for that week. I can't remember what it was now. But she raised an eyebrow and told me that she doubted she'd ever return.

"After the service that next Sunday, as I was out shaking hands with people again, I saw her. I wasn't looking for her. I didn't really expect to see her again. She was standing by our information booth, handling a Bible. I wanted to signal to the woman working the booth not to let the young lady get away, to make sure she was given a free Bible. We've got good staff. I didn't have to do anything. When Nancy came through the line to talk to me, she had a new Bible and some literature tucked under her arm.

"I didn't want to make too big a deal out of her returning, you know, like by thanking her for coming back. So I just asked what she thought of the message. This time she smiled and said she'd enjoyed it. She was confused but thought she understood what I was trying to say. And the rest, as they say, is history. She started coming to church on Sundays and midweek services every Wednesday night. She was saved and baptized later that same year. About five years ago I needed a new administrative assistant and she needed work."

Again, I began to wonder if there had been a relationship between Ross and Nancy. He seemed very taken by her. If she was anything like Stacey, I could understand the attraction, but Ross was a married man.

Regardless, I had more information and a few additional pieces to add to my puzzle. Now all I had to do was try and make them fit. I didn't like jigsaw puzzles. Too many of the tiny cutouts looked identical, yet each piece was just different enough to serve its own purpose. When I was younger I knew how to force a square peg down a round hole. Unadulterated force.

"Was she part of New Forest?" I asked.

"She never said," Pastor Ross answered. "And I never pushed for answers."

"What about the graffiti? You think it's linked?"

"Like you said, it's got to be."

"So what do we do?" I asked.

"We can't go to the police," he said. "There has to be someone else we can go to for help. The press?"

I shook my head. "I don't know. Maybe."

"I need to think about this. I need to pray," Pastor Ross said.

"I think we need to act," I said. "I've been praying all along, and it's only gotten me deeper and deeper into this mess." I looked at Alan. "You sure this is the line of work you want to get into?"

He stood up. "It's my calling," he said.

I shook my head as I walked out of the office.

I drove by New Forest Church. The facility was a modern warehouse with white siding, windows set up high, and a big marble-crafted sign on the front lawn that kind of resembled a tombstone. Parking was behind the building.

The one thing that stood out was another sign. This one was on a pole and impaled into the earth near the front doors. It boasted that the property was protected by M.S.S., Monroe Security Systems.

Instant idea. I dialed my phone. "Tay?" I said, when he answered. "Remember Felix? You still have his number? Great. See if you can get him to meet us for coffee or something today. I don't care when, as long as it's today. Call me when you set it up." He wanted to know what was going on. "I'm on my way over. I'll fill you in as soon as I get there."

Chapter Thirty-six

As I drove toward Tay's, I repeatedly tried to reach Stacey. The battery of her cell phone had to be dead, or the thing was turned off, or broken. I tried to stay calm. This was coincidental, nothing more.

Coincidences happened, like if I'd unexpectedly run into Tay at the mall. That would be a coincidence. The fact that Nancy was a witch-turned-Christian and was now possibly being held captive by a Wiccan church, and the fact that the Farrars were ticked at me for going to the police, and the fact that Stacey wasn't answering her cell phone all of a sudden amounted to more than mere coincidence.

It was a bit much to accept, too much to swallow. The more time that passed without hearing from her, the more I worried that something might be wrong—seriously wrong.

Taking my focus off Stacey wasn't easy, but right now I concentrated on Nancy. Pastor Ross had unleashed a flood of information—more than I'd been ready for—information that I hadn't expected to hear. Though strange and eerie, things started to make a little sense. I didn't understand much, but I could see how those puzzle pieces might fit together.

If Nancy had been a witch, I wondered if part of her was still faithful to that belief system. Maybe she felt Christianity wasn't working out and had backslid into her old ways. It was a possibility. I found it hard to believe that after being exposed to the good news, one could turn away from God, but I bet it happened all the time.

If Nancy had decided to skip out on Christianity in order to return to paganism and witchcraft, one thing didn't make sense. One piece of the puzzle didn't fit.

Dane. The young girl who'd come to see me at Phoebe's and told me that New Forest wasn't all it seemed. She'd indicated that Nancy was being held like a prisoner against her will. I had no reason *not* to believe Dane. She was a kid, sure, but something disturbed her enough that she went out of her way in an attempt to do the right thing. She'd notified me.

My cell rang; it way Tay. "What's going on?" I said, answering the phone.

"Felix will meet us downtown for lunch. You want to pick me up?" Tay said.

"More than halfway there already," I said.

Charlie's was crowded. King sat at his usual table, back to the wall, eyes constantly roaming, scanning the activity in the bar. He didn't like surprises. To avoid them, he always had to be ready, whether it meant being ready to slip out the back door or take a stand.

Tay and I played pool against Bones and Felix.

Felix was about thirty-five years old, weighed two-fifty, stood just over six feet tall, and had big, dark eyes that were encircled by a seemingly permanent bloodshot-stained sclera. Due to the size of his bulging biceps, he was able to house an abundance of tattoos.

Cigarette smoke filled the room. Loud rap music with explicit lyrics riddled with sex, violence, and hatred pulsated like an actual living entity within the bar, a parasite that didn't feed off of the patrons but nourished us instead. To compete with the volume of the music, people shouted, trying to talk louder over all the noise just to be heard. That combination, along with the beer and whiskey I'd downed on an empty stomach, contributed to the throbbing headache that insisted on trying to pound multiple holes through my skull. I kept closing my eyes, afraid that eventually they would pop out of their sockets.

We mostly shot pool for drinks. Loser buys a round. Tonight, Bones and Felix were shelling out the cash. Tay and I were beating them in less time than it took for me to finish a beer. I could use a break. We wouldn't stop playing, though, for one reason: other people waited to play. As long as we kept playing, we were making a statement to everyone in the bar: *We don't play by the rules and there's nothing you can do about it.*

After Tay sank the eight ball, securing another victory for our team, Felix made his way up to the bar, a wad of bills in hand. As I racked up the balls for another game, I noticed that King was talking on his cell phone. As he ended his call he motioned to get Bones' attention.

"Boss wants you," I said.

Bones leaned his cue stick against the pool table and sauntered over to King, shouldering his way through anyone who was in his direct path. I paid attention to their exchange. I couldn't hear what was said between them. I sure didn't know how to read lips, but I knew it was business. King had a job. Soon, Bones would return to the pool table and dole out an assignment.

At the moment, I needed aspirin and some sleep. Not work. "I don't feel like going out tonight," I said.

"Ditto," Tay said from the barstool where he sat. He tapped the padded end of his cue stick on the floor.

Felix returned, handing over fresh, cold beers. "Thanks," I said, setting it on the table next to my other half-full beer, still cold.

"What do we got?" Felix asked. When he said this, it sounded more like two words: "Whadawe got?"

I shrugged. "King wanted to see Bones."

"I don't feel much like going out tonight," he said.

"Join the club," Tay responded.

Without staring, we all watched Bones step away from King. His playful Friday night mood looked suddenly sullen. His eyes narrowed, his jaw tensed, and there was a don't-mess-with-me bounce that only showed up in his step when King gave out work.

"Murphy's got money stashed in his attic," Bones said, as if we all knew exactly what he was talking about.

"Who's Murphy?" Tay asked.

"He's into King for nearly sixty grand," Bones said. "He took out loans after losing a bundle on lousy college basketball bets. Those kids aren't predictable enough to wager serious cash. People don't care."

"B and E?" Felix asked.

Nodding, Bones said, "No one should be home. He's supposed to work nights as a production supervisor for that film company—used to be a real big company, I can't think of the name right now."

"I know the one you mean," I said. I didn't, but what difference did it make? The guy had a job, big deal. It wasn't like King could have his wages garnished to get back the sixty Gs.

"Yeah, anyway, so no one should be home. We break and enter and search the place, starting with the attic. King got a tip from some other sap, a guy who works with Murphy, about money being in the attic," Bones said.

"How'd King get a hold of the snitch?" Felix asked.

"Seems he doesn't know how to place a winning bet, either, and he's into King for some bills, too, but nothing as weighty as what Murphy owes, so King had a deal cut. The snitch found out some stuff about Murphy, and King reduced the snitch's debt by half," Bones explained. "And Tommy, no matter what we find, King wants you to track down Murphy, teach him a thing or two about manners and respect. King was not very happy that Murphy never returned any of his calls. You see what I'm saying?"

I knew exactly what needed to be done. "Consider it done."

"Felix, Murphy's home has a security system. Problem?" Bones asked.

"Doubt it. I got my tools in the car," he said.

"Always prepared," Tay said. "Like a good little Boy Scout."

We gathered our stuff and nodded a good-bye to the boss as we walked out of Charlie's.

Tay and I met Felix at some all-you-can-eat Mexican buffet on State Street. It sat just across the street from the federal courthouse, sandwiched in between an adult bookstore and a shoe repair place. It was dimly lit, and I wasn't completely comfortable trusting the quality of food I was about to ingest there. Living dangerously, the three of us walked the buffet line, filling out plates with enchiladas, hard tacos, and quesadillas.

"I love it here, man," Felix said, crunching into a taco. Ground beef and diced tomatoes dropped out the opposite end of the taco onto his plate. Except that he now weighed close to three hundred, and a lot of his muscle looked more like flab, he'd not changed much over the years. The whites of his eyes were as bloodshot red as ever. "I just love it. For awhile all you could find were Chinese buffet places on every corner. Don't get me wrong. I like Chinese. Love it. I just needed a break. Some variety."

I raised my eyebrows. "This is different."

Felix nodded and smiled and looked around as if I'd just complimented him on his ethnic diversity. He told us how M.S.S. had hired him out of prison. He'd broken into so many homes and businesses sporting an M.S.S. system that, if they couldn't stop him, they would put him on payroll. He worked with design engineer teams. They created what they considered foolproof systems and wanted to see if Felix could find a way to penetrate them. Felix claimed he always found a way to bypass the alarms—always. It infuriated the design engineers but also inspired them to redouble their efforts. "It's a great job," he said.

"Speaking of jobs, I've got one for you," I said. I wasn't here to eat. This was a working lunch, as far as I was concerned.

Felix sat up straight and, for the first time since sitting down, seemed to ignore his food. "Look, guys. Tay, you told me you two were Christians now. I don't do jobs anymore. I mean, since Bones and King killed each other, I've been pretty clean.

For the most part. I got a good thing at M.S.S. I don't want to do anything that might jeopardize my career."

This was going to be tougher than I thought. Felix seemed solid. I didn't want to be the one responsible for tainting that. I felt my cause was righteous. Stacey and Nancy needed help. The police thought Tay and I were crazy, so we couldn't count on them for help. If anything was going to get done, we had to do it ourselves.

As best I could and as quickly as possible, I recapped the entire story again—for the umpteenth time this week. Felix ate the whole time I talked. Twice I had to put myself on pause while he ran back up through the buffet line and replenished his plate.

When I finished, I thought for sure I'd wasted my time, that he'd not heard a word I'd said, was more concerned about enjoying his free lunch and keeping his nose clean.

"That it?" Felix asked.

Tay and I exchanged glances, then nodded at each other.

"Pretty much," I said. I almost started defending everything, but I held my tongue.

"So you want me to help the two of you sneak into New Forest Church, bypassing their M.S.S. security system?" Felix asked for clarification.

Again, I nodded.

"Sure." Felix patted his stomach. "I might go up for just a bit more," he said, eyeing his empty plate suspiciously, as if someone else might have finished the food, explaining how he could still possibly be hungry.

"Wait, did you say, 'sure,' you'd help?" I asked.

"Yeah, exactly. Sure," Felix said, standing up.

"But what about being clean all this time?" Tay said.

"And not wanting to do anything that might jeopardize your career?" I said. "What about all that?"

"I mean, yeah, that's all true and everything, but, man, I'm bored, you know? And it seems like you guys are doing this for some really good—albeit weird—reasons. How can I say no? You need help. You came to me. I'd never turn you guys away. Besides, I'm not going to do the B and E. You two are. I'll work it from M.S.S.," he said. "Now, who could use a few more tacos?"

Against our better judgment, Tay and I joined Felix for another pass through the buffet line. We settled in at our booth and enjoyed the rest of our lunch as we began to flesh out a plan of attack.

Thomas Phillips

As soon as we left the buffet, I tried to reach Officer Stratton on my cell phone but settled for leaving him a voice mail message. I told him I wanted to drop the complaint I'd filed. I explained that I didn't willfully file a false complaint, but it was all too possible that I'd overreacted and should have refrained from calling the police in the first place.

"Okay," I said. "That's done."

"You know what I was just thinking?" Tay asked.

"What?"

"We plan on breaking in to this church tonight, right? But they're witches and warlocks. They come out at night and sleep all day, don't they?"

"That's vampires," I pointed out.

"You know what I'm talking about," Tay said. He was serious and not in the mood for my sarcasm.

"No, it's a good point. Maybe we should watch the place tonight, stake out, you know? And then if we see that the place stays quiet, we hit them Sunday night," I offered reluctantly. I did not want to waste more time. I was ready for action. There was no telling what kind of danger Stacey and Nancy were in, and as hard as I tried to control my mind, my imagination was getting the better of me.

The ~~molEch~~ Prophecy

"Okay, but what if Sunday nights are the nights they stay late? Tommy, you know the deal on this type of job. We watch the place for awhile to see what's happening. This is all so spur-of-the-moment," he said. He was right.

"We don't have the time."

"It's risky."

"You know, you've already done more than any friend could ever hope," I said. "This could get really rough and messy. Just because I think that what we're doing is righteous doesn't mean the police will if they nab us for breaking and entering. You want out, I'll understand and respect that decision. I can promise you that the friendship won't suffer, either."

Tay was silent for a moment. Perhaps thinking. I'd give him all the time he needed. There was no point in pushing. He could answer when he was ready. And just when I was going to tell him as much, he opened his mouth.

"A good friend will come and bail you out of jail," he said.

"That's right, man. That's a good friend."

"But a true friend will be sitting next to you saying, 'Man, wasn't that fun?'"

I looked over at Tay, not expecting to see such a big smirk spread across his lips. "You just make that up?" I asked.

"Nah. Got it in one of those chain-letter e-mails. Got to admit, it sounds almost biblical, doesn't it?" he said. "We're more than true friends, man. We're brothers. Don't you know that by now?"

We locked our right hands in a handshake.

"Yeah, I know it. I know it," I said.

CHAPTER THIRTY-SEVEN

We stopped at Tay's for a pair of binoculars. Things were moving fast. Tay and I were hours away from breaking into a church. We were a heartbeat away from committing a felony. God didn't just point you in the right direction, and if you veered, reach down and straighten you out. Not physically, anyway. While still in Tay's house, we took a moment to stop and pray for guidance, strength, and courage.

"Feeling naked?" Tay asked as he pulled the binoculars out of the case and looked them over.

I knew what he meant. Heat. Like we should be packing. "I can't remember the last time I even handled a gun," I said. It was a lie. I fired it three inches to the left of a guy's head, demanding that he fork over the money he owed King. I never meant for the bullet to get that close. I almost killed the man. The guy, who'd wet himself, handed over all that he had. It wasn't even close to enough. I saw it in his eyes. He thought I meant to kill him. He wasn't holding out. I was too shaken to care. I took what he gave me and got out of there. "We don't need them, anyway," I added.

"Amen to that," Tay said.

We drove out to New Forest and parked under the mini-mart sign that advertised the cost of gasoline, just across and down the street some from the church. Tay had the binoculars out and was using them to zoom in on the church property. "These work pretty well," he said. "I've never used them before."

"What'd you buy them for?" I asked.

"After I won the lottery I ended up buying a lot of things I always wanted but never ended up using."

"You always wanted binoculars?" I said as he handed them over. I held them up to my eyes. "Oh yeah, and these are nice." I could adjust the focus so that the front door was as crisp an image as if it were two feet from my face. I found the back of the church and could zoom in close enough to see fuzzy dice dangling from a rearview mirror in a car parked in the back lot.

"When you look through those, do you see one big circle or two almost-full circles?" Tay asked.

"You mean, like in the movies, when they show you what some army guy sees when he looks through binoculars?" I asked. "And we see two circles, one for each eye—where they kind of blend together where our nose would be?"

"Yeah. Is that what you see?"

"Nah. I see one big circle. You?"

"Me, too."

I gave him back the binoculars. From where we were parked, I could see the front door of the church just fine. However, if someone went through the door, I would never be able to see what the person looked like. Not from this distance.

"I don't see any external security cameras," he said. That helped. "When you get in for a closer look, keep an eye out for cameras in the back."

"Felix said they didn't have any on their account with M.S.S.," I reminded him.

"That doesn't mean a thing. We need to be alert," Tay said. He knew what he was talking about.

"Can't tell from here how many cars are behind the church," I said. "At some point, maybe when it gets darker, I'll have to run over there for a closer look."

Tay didn't argue with me, nor did he volunteer to go look himself.

"When's the last time you tried calling Stacey?" Tay asked.

I pulled out my cell phone and dialed. Nothing. "They got her, Tay. I can feel it."

"This is all a bit creepy," he said.

"Tell me about it," I said. "Something's going on. I'm afraid to think what, but Alex Farrar is up to something."

"And we're going to stop him?"

"You're not supposed to say that like a question. You have to have a little conviction, man," I scolded. "Like this: 'And we're going to stop him!'"

Tay laughed. I laughed.

We talked for another hour. The sun dropped quickly. It was nearly four o'clock and as dark as midnight. Unreal. There was absolutely no activity at the church.

I ran into the mini-mart and bought some beef jerky and slushies, blue for Tay, red for me.

"I still can't believe you won't drink anything blue," Tay said, laughing.

"I won't," I said, shaking my head.

"Are you afraid of having a blue tongue?" he asked, sticking his blue tongue out at me.

"It could be part of it. I don't know. I just don't like to eat or drink anything blue," I said, provoking another outburst of laughter. "But I read somewhere that more people avoid eating or drinking things that are blue than any other color."

"You mean there are more people like you than people who are afraid to eat things that are yellow?" Tay said, almost laughing too hard to speak.

"I think the article said that blue is a color asso-ciated with poison."

"You making this up?"

"I just told you it was in some article."

"Right," Tay teased.

I chose to ignore him and graciously sipped my red slushie.

At ten after six, a young woman appeared from behind the back of the church. She climbed into the car with the fuzzy dice, started the engine, and pulled out of the parking lot like someone with some serious Saturday night plans.

"All right," I said. "I'm going to sneak over. You see anything odd, honk the horn."

Now it felt real.

"You want these?" he offered the binoculars.

"Nah," I said, initially. "You know what, yeah. Let me take them just in case I can get a peek in a window or something."

I felt it. Adrenaline. My heart beat fast and hard. It had been years since I had felt a level of adrena-line as high as this. Most people never experienced a true surge of adrenaline. Sure, they get sweaty palms and quick, shallow breathing when they watch some horror flick. And maybe they get close to what I'm feeling right now if they have to walk to their car in a dark, deserted parking lot—and they've just heard the unmistakable noise that signals they're not alone.

Still, watching a movie or walking to your car is different because, despite the energy your body creates so you can react to the danger, you choose to be trapped in fear. You either cover your eyes and scream at the movie or hold your keys like knives in the fists of your shaking hands.

I was different. I liked adrenaline. I fed on it. It was like a drug, an old addiction.

After crossing the street, I stayed in the shadows. I didn't try to hide. That draws attention. When you act like you belong, even if you are in the middle of nowhere, people ignore you. No matter how sneaky someone thinks he is, someone else is always watching. The second you duck behind a corner, that someone will see you—and more than likely will call the police.

As I approached the rear of the church, I could see that the parking lot was empty. I stayed as deep in the shadows as I could while walking as casually as I could. Other than a blue dumpster and what looked like a large tool shed in the far corner, there was nothing else there. I did not see any external security cameras.

The back of the building was windowless, except for a rectangle of glass on each of the double doors. I went up to one, cupped my hands, and looked inside. The place was not completely dark. I saw two computer monitors lit with screen savers. It looked like a hall light might be on, too.

When my cell phone rang, I jumped back from the doors, certain I'd set off an alarm. For a moment it felt like my heart had quit beating on me altogether, and it took a couple of seconds for me to catch my breath and fish my cell out of my pocket. "Hello?" I said.

"Have you called off the police?" a voice asked.

"It's done. I want to talk to Stacey," I demanded. "And Nancy!"

"I'll be in touch," he said, and ended the call.

I could not figure out why Alex was insistent on trying to disguise his voice. The game was up. He was going to be arrested and charged with kidnapping. There was no way around it. Once Stacey and her sister were freed, the police would come for him. He had to realize that. That's what happened to kidnappers. They got arrested.

Kidnappers.

Usually, kidnappers wanted something. Alex hadn't asked for anything. Yet.

As I slowly made my way back the way I'd come, I heard a horn honking. The horn kept honking as I came around the rear of the church.

The horn. Tay's warning.

I saw the headlights bouncing on the pavement

and stepped behind the building. Where could I hide? There it was. The big blue dumpster. I raced for it and dove just as the car I'd seen approaching came to a screeching halt. I heard doors opening and people talking in loud whispers, using harsh tones. I peered around the dumpster. Two men. One could be Alex. The other jingled a set of keys. I couldn't see or hear anything really. They entered the church.

I stayed low as I made my way through the well-lit lot. There were no shadows for blending. I was exposed, so I moved fast. Once off church property, my breathing returned to normal. I didn't think I'd been seen, but I hadn't really seen anything, either. And with people inside the church, Tay and I would have to sit and wait even longer before going in.

Chapter Thirty-eight

Around eight, the people who had entered New Forest left. At nine, under the cover of darkness, Tay and I crossed the street from where we were parked and ran toward the church. We were going in. I had Felix on the cell phone. He was at M.S.S., sitting by a switchboard.

"We've got to make this quick," he said. "You go in, you get out. Minutes."

"Relax." I wore a wireless earpiece tied to the cell phone in my pocket. I needed my hands free. "We're almost to the door."

As we made our way to the back of the church, all I could hear was the sound of our shoes crunching against loose gravel. It sounded like firecrackers going off under my feet, or it just seemed that loud because I was that nervous. This wasn't me anymore. Breaking and entering. What was I doing? What was I dragging Tay into?

"Tay," I said.

"We're cool," he said, as if he'd been reading my

thoughts. "These women are missing, man. We're cool."

Right. We're cool, I thought as we reached the back door. "Felix?" I said.

"Right here, guys."

"We're at the door." I held my breath.

"System's disengaged," he said.

I signaled Tay, who unzipped a small, black leather pouch. He pulled out a set of pick-like tools that reminded me of something my dentist might have used while performing oral surgery. He got down to work, inserting the picks into the lock, twisting and clicking them. "Well?" I asked.

"Give me a second," Tay said. "It's been awhile."

It seemed like ten minutes before I heard the click and release of the lock. Tay looked up at me, a huge grin on his face. "I kind of forgot how satisfying that can feel," he said.

I opened the door. "Don't get used to it," I said. "Felix, we're in."

"Minutes, guys. I'm giving you minutes. Do not mess anything up in there. You've got your gloves on?"

"We're wearing gloves," I promised. The little bit of light from the glowing computer monitors helped, but we had penlights that we switched on and kept aimed at the ground.

The mo|Ech Prophecy

We were looking for one of two things. Nancy or Stacey was one. And if they weren't here, we hoped to find some indication of where they might be. We'd both decided that if the women were being held in the building, and held against their wills, they'd be kept somewhere secluded, like in the basement.

Doing a quick search of the main level, we realized we could not make out a lot of detail. It was too dark. The church put a lot of money into statues. For the most part, they were formless, hulking shadows. Eerily, they stood silent guard in every corner. Thankfully, I could not see anything specific.

Office doors lined one hallway. None of them were locked. We peeked in and then moved on. The sanctuary was not as big as I'd expected, especially based on the overall size of the facility. The stage platform was pentagon shaped and sat in the center of the room. Rows of pews, like something you'd find in a traditional church, came out from each side of the pentagon stage, each one slightly longer than the one in front of it, creating five aisles between the rows.

We found the kitchen, what appeared to be classrooms, a conference room, and a storage room. But no Nancy and no Stacey.

"How we looking, guys?" Felix asked. "You've been in there just over three minutes."

"Nothing on the first level," I said.

"How do you know there's more than one level?" Felix asked. Good question.

"We don't. Give us two more minutes, two," I said. I turned to Tay. "We've got to find a stairway."

We ran back through the place, checking each room more thoroughly, looking for doorways that opened up to more than just a closet. Nothing.

"You know, I saw a movie once," Tay said, leading me back to the sanctuary, where we made a beeline toward center stage. "And in the movie—" He stood on the stage and began to tap his foot on the carpeted surface until his foot hit an area that sounded hollow. We dropped to our knees.

"One minute," Felix warned.

"Two more," I begged. "We might have found something."

We used our penlights together to inspect the carpet more closely. There had to be a cutaway, a handle, a rope, a doorknob, something. There wasn't.

We sat on the edge of the stage, defeated. "I don't know what to tell you," Tay said.

"It's too bad we can't just lift the stage," I said.

Tay looked at me, shaking his head. We stood

up, grabbed a corner of the stage and lifted. One section of the pentagon, the section with the hollow sound, opened. It was a doorway. We shined our lights down into the darkness. The tiny beams did little to infiltrate the gloom below.

"I'm freaked," I admitted.

"Ditto, man."

I saw stairs and went down first, descending into what I was confident held certain doom. Upstairs, I had worried about police seeing our flashlight beams shining this way and that, which was why we'd kept them aimed at the floor. Now, I didn't care. I aimed my light all over the place. The power the tiny light carried was insignificant.

"I thought there'd be lit torches or something," I said.

Tay laughed. "Whisper, man."

"Ten seconds," Felix said.

"We found the basement," I said.

"It's time to go, guys. You have to get out," Felix ordered.

I shut the earpiece off. "I just cut Felix off," I told Tay.

"Is he telling us it's time to go?"

"Yep," I said.

"How long have we been in the church?" Tay asked.

"Ten minutes."

"He's right then. We need to get out of here."

"And we will," I promised, reaching the bottom of the stairs. I felt along the wall and was amazed when my fingers fumbled over a row of light switches. "Lights."

"Might as well," Tay said.

I switched them on, wondering what the light would possibly reveal in this pit.

Filing cabinets, storage trays, big desks, old computers, some broken chairs.

"You expect prison cells with big wood doors and iron bars in the small windows?" Tay asked.

"More or less," I said.

"Let's get out of here," Tay said.

I walked out to the center of the basement, looking around one last time, not ready to submit to defeat. "There's a door," I said. It was in the right-hand corner at the back of the room.

"We've got to get out of here," Tay said.

"Two seconds," I said. I needed something. There had to be something.

I pulled on the door, half expecting it to be locked. It opened.

"Tay, take a look at this," I said. Tay joined me in the doorway. It was an office with red carpeting, bookshelves, a laptop, a mahogany desk, and a big-screen television set. "It's something," I said.

"It sure is, but what? I mean, why have an office hidden down here?"

"Exactly. Something important is down here. Something someone doesn't want everyone else to know about," I said. The trouble was *what*.

I walked into the room.

"That's odd," I said. It was a solitary book sitting open on a podium in the center of the room. I walked up to the book. Journal entries. A red-tasseled bookmark lay across the pages. I closed the book and looked at the cover. It was a jacketless hardcover with no title on the binding at all. Nothing indicated who had authored the journal. It was more than three-quarters full, I noticed as I flipped through the pages. I went back to the bookmarked page and looked more closely at what it had been opened up to.

"What's this about?" Tay asked.

At the bottom of the second page was a drawing of a pregnant woman on some kind of altar. Robed people stood around the woman, one ready to accept delivery of the baby. Two words were written under the drawing: *Unto Molech*. I tried reading what was written on the other pages. It was in Shakespearean-like language.

"It says here something about once the baby is brought to full term, it must be delivered on the night of a new moon—a time normally reserved for witches and warlocks to spend in meditation. Then it says something about a child born of good and evil will rise to great power and free those who have been long-suffering. I don't know. I don't get it," I said. I flipped back a page. We read.

"What's this about handfasting?" Tay asked.

"I don't know. The picture shows that couple with their hands tied together with—is that supposed to be a snake?"

"Looks like it. What's handfasting?"

"No clue. I can't really understand this, not here, not trying to read it now," I said. I needed to read it more slowly, more closely.

"We've got to get out of here," Tay said.

I dialed Felix. "Hey, we got disconnected."

"I'm giving you two seconds to get out, and then I'm switching on the security system, regardless," Felix said.

"This does not sound like the bored man I had lunch with," I teased.

"This was more than enough excitement for me. I guess I'm kind of used to not being in prison!" He yelled in my ear.

"I'm taking the book," I said.

Tay grabbed my arm. "You take the book and they'll know someone's been here."

"This could be important."

"And it might just be some worthless diary. Leave it."

Tay was right. This book might not lead us anywhere. I wasn't a thief—not anymore. We shut off the basement lights, ran back up the stairs, closed the doorway in the stage, and made our way toward the back door—just as headlights lit up the parking lot.

"Felix, someone's here." Tay and I jogged—keeping low—toward the front door.

"It's locked," Tay said, pushing on it.

"Work on it," I said and headed for the back door. Two men got out of a car. It might have been the same two from earlier. They stood talking over the hood. "Hurry!" I urged.

As the two men walked away from the car, I ran back to Tay. "They're coming," I said. "And one of them is definitely Alex."

Tay's leather pouch stuck out of his back pocket. He worked his tools in the lock. He held his penlight in his mouth, clenched between his teeth, and aimed at the lock.

"Guys?" It was Felix.

"We're almost out of here," I said quietly.

"And the people coming in?" Felix asked.

"We have seconds," I told Tay.

"I'm going to have to activate the alarm," Felix warned.

"Felix—you've got to give us a chance."

I heard keys disengage the backdoor lock.

Then Tay sighed. "I got it," he said, pushing open the door.

We ran out into the night. "Set the alarm, Felix," I said as Tay and I sprinted across the street to my car. We climbed in, shut the doors, and sat there panting. I felt frantic. "Felix?"

"We're good. I activated the alarm, and ten seconds later it was disengaged using the keypad code by whoever entered the church," Felix explained. "Nothing out of the ordinary."

"Yeah," Tay said, "except the front door's not locked. They're bound to find that suspicious once it's discovered."

Tay was right. But we were out. As far as we knew, they did not have any video surveillance. We had left everything in order. They were more likely to suspect that the last person out of the building that night had forgotten to lock the door. At least, I hoped that's what they'd think.

Chapter Thirty-nine

"Now what?" Tay asked. We were sitting in my car in a parking lot across from New Forest Church. Breaking into the church hadn't been one of my better ideas. We'd narrowly escaped. I just didn't know where else to turn. Everything I tried kept leading me to nothing. Empty. Zilch.

"We could follow Alex," Tay suggested.

"We could. But we're not. I'm taking you home. We've had enough excitement for one night," I said. I was putting my foot down. From here on, I was working alone. If we'd gotten caught inside New Forest, we'd have been locked away in a real prison for sure. We already knew the police weren't buying any of this. New Forest would press charges. If I told the truth, I'd sound crazy, lending credibility to what I'm sure the police already thought of me.

"But Stacey and Nancy," Tay said.

"We're done for the night," I reiterated. "We almost got caught."

"But we didn't."

"Not the point. I'm losing my grip here. This isn't our job. This isn't our responsibility. We need to go back to the police and keep telling them our story until someone listens. That's what we need to do. We're acting like we're in a movie or something. We're not. It's real. We're not supersleuths. We're not going to rescue the damsels in distress at the very last moment. If we keep acting the way we're acting, we'll wind up either in trouble with the police, hurt, or worse."

"There they go," Tay said, pointing to a car pulling out of the New Forest parking lot.

"We're not following anyone," I said. The car made a right, sped up, but then stopped for a red light.

"They're going to get away."

"We're not following anyone. I'm taking you home." I started the engine.

I pulled into traffic and made a right at the light. "I live the other way," Tay said.

I couldn't believe I was doing this. I didn't even have enough sense to listen to my own good sense. "Shortcut," I said to Tay. He smiled and tightened his seatbelt.

"You got your cell?" Tay asked. I fished it out of

my pocket and handed it to him. He dialed. "Lea-trice? It's Tay. We're good, baby. It's *all* good. Can you do me a favor? You on the Internet? What's it say about handfasting?" I looked over at Tay and winked. "Good idea," I said.

We were several car lengths behind Alex, headed west on Latta Road. I didn't need to get any closer to keep an eye on him. He drove evenly, which I didn't expect. Knowing he was a rocker, I expected him to have a lead foot. Stereotyping was often a big downfall for me.

Worried about Stacey, I concentrated on the road. If I allowed myself too much time to think about where she might be or how she might be, I would only end up upsetting myself. I knew she was all right. She had to be all right. I was going to find her. I was going to rescue her. I knew this was not a movie. This was real life.

I thought I loved Stacey. It was hard to know for sure. I'd never been in love with a woman before. I'd never felt this way. I wanted to be around her, to hold her hand. I wanted to look in her eyes, listen to her talk. I wanted to share parts of my life with her, parts I'd never shared with anyone else before—not even Tay. This was why I thought it was love. And if it wasn't love, it didn't matter. I loved the way it felt.

Except now, I desperately needed to find her.

"Handfasting, yeah," Tay said. He pulled the phone away from his face. "I put you on speaker, Leatrice. Tell Tommy what you just told me."

"Hey, Tommy," she said.

"Hiya, Leatrice."

"Handfasting. It's an ancient Celtic wedding ceremony. It's a ritual where the bride and groom have their hands tied together. It's where the term *tying the knot* comes from," she said.

I looked at Tay. "Is there going to be a wedding?"

"Nancy's pregnant," Tay pointed out.

"Maybe Alex is the father?" I said. "And they're going to get married? Could that be it? Could that be all this was? We're seconds away from crashing a wedding?"

"A handfasting," Tay corrected.

I nodded in agreement.

"Thanks, dear," Tay said to Leatrice, and ended his call.

"Oh man," I said, pounding the steering wheel. "I wasn't paying attention to Alex. He's not in front of me anymore."

My church was coming up on the right. The parking lot was empty. Only a few cars were ahead of me, and none belonged to Alex.

"Let's get some coffee and talk," Tay suggested.

I turned around. We headed in the opposite direction, toward Dewey and Java Brew, the place where Stacey and I first met for coffee. As I drove, I kept my eye out for Alex's car. We parked at Java Brew, went in, and ordered. Taking a seat at a table against the wall, we sat for a moment, playing around with the stir straws in our cups of coffee.

"That journal was important," I finally said, breaking the silence.

"You couldn't just take it."

"I know. You're right." I turned my chair so I could lean back and rest my head against the wall. "I just wanted more time to read it, you know. It was written in Old English or whatever. I hate that. I can't even imagine people talking that way."

"You got a better look at it than I did. I just saw the pictures," Tay said.

"You're a good friend, you know that?"

"Brothers," he said. We shook hands over the table. "We'll find them."

"I know we will."

"Do you? I'm not sure you do."

"I'm trying to be extremely optimistic, I think." I looked at Tay, who was staring at me. "How come you're so confident?"

He pointed up to the ceiling. "Need I say more?"

I smiled, secretly admitting to myself that I didn't share his level of trust. "Something bothers me, though—about the journal."

"That you couldn't tell who wrote it?" he asked.

"No. I mean, yeah. That's weird, but that isn't it. It's something else. Something I saw or read. But I can't think of it, not clearly. It's like right there," I said, leaning forward and sticking my tongue out, pointing it at the tip. I sat back and crossed my arms. "I'm missing something. It was right there. And now it's gone."

My cell rang. I pulled it out of my pocket and fumbled, spinning it around in my hands. I wanted to see it was Stacey calling. It wasn't. I handed the phone over to Tay. "It's Leatrice."

He answered. "Yeah, doll? We're at Java Brew. I don't know, hold on," he said. "She wants me to put it on speaker. We could keep the volume low?" He set the phone down in the center of the table. We both leaned in close. "It's on speaker."

"I did some more searching on the Internet," Leatrice said. "I used a lot more words in the search, making it more specific. I included wedding, pregnant, Farrar, baby, and handfasting, and I came up with several interesting things."

"Man, you are *it*, Leatrice. You know what I'm saying? You are *it*," I said, grinning broadly. "You can't let this one get away," I said to Tay.

"You tell him, Tommy. I'm a keeper," she agreed.

The mo|Ech Prophecy

"Who's arguing?" Tay said, his defensive ploy.

"So what'd you find?" I asked.

"Gerald Farrar," Leatrice said.

"Alex's father," I said.

"Right. He's written a number of articles in print and online. We're not just talking about tabloid publications, either. We're talking about respectable publications like *Popular Science*, *National Review*, and the *New York Times*," she said. She talked fast. She was breathing hard, clearly excited. "There's one article, "The Becoming," that was published in multiple publications. I didn't read it all—or any of them, for that matter—but I was able to get this gist of it. Basically, Farrar has a Wicca coven that believes a new master is coming and will be born during this decade. It talks about the birth parents being like night and day. I'm not sure what that means. It doesn't say. If that isn't weird enough for you, it gets loopier. Apparently, once the child is born, he's to be offered to Molech."

"Molech. That's it!" I interrupted. "The journal we saw. Under the one picture, where the baby was being born, it said Molech-something, or something-Molech."

"It's in the Bible," Tay said.

"The Ammonites and Canaanites worshipped him," Leatrice added. "He was one of their gods.

The people sacrificed their firstborn babies to him. They burned their children in a fire."

"They put the infant in the outstretched arms of the Molech statue and started a fire under the child, who was slowly burned alive," Tay said. "King Solomon—David's son—erected a statue to this god, too. And Solomon was one of the good guys from the Bible."

"It was Josiah who finally saw how evil all of this was, worshipping gods and goddesses other than the one true God. He had the statues destroyed," Leatrice said.

"So Gerald Farrar expects Nancy to marry him and have his baby—considering that they are somehow 'night' and 'day'—because this baby is going to be some all-powerful master, only then they plan to burn him as a sacrifice to Molech?" It didn't make sense.

"Not exactly. Farrar believes that the baby will survive the fire. He thinks the baby won't die. That's how they will know that he is their new leader—*their* savior, he calls him at one point. What will follow is a reign of persecution and suffering for Christians. This kid is something like the Antichrist," she said.

"And he'll be born in Rochester, New York?" I mocked. No one laughed.

The molEch Prophecy

"It doesn't mean he is going to be the Antichrist. I mean, it doesn't say that. It just promises the beginning of a reign of persecution for all Christians," she said. "And one more thing. Handfasting ceremonies need to take place at midnight on the night of a waxing crescent moon."

"What's a waxing crescent moon?" I asked.

"It's when the moon starts to look like a Cheshire cat grin, as the moon is growing each night toward reaching a full moon. And boys, there's one tonight—a waxing crescent moon."

I looked at my phone for the time. It was eleven o'clock. "You think Nancy's going to get married tonight?"

"It's possible," Leatrice said.

It's possible, sure, but where?

"You know what we're not considering here?" I asked. "What if she wants to get married? What if she left Faith Community Church and quit being a Christian because she's in love with someone from New Forest and just so happens to be having his baby? She willingly quit her job and moved out of her apartment. Who are we to interfere with her life?"

"What about the baby?"

"Come on, this Farrar guy and his cult may be different and a bit scary, but we're in the twenty-first century here. He's not going to sacrifice a child. He has to know, despite what he's written, that if you set a child on fire, that child is going to die. What parent—I don't care how hateful a person they are—will burn their child alive?" It didn't make sense to me.

"What about people who beat their kids, or put their cigarettes out on a child's arm?" Leatrice asked. "My father used to do that to me."

I stared silently at the phone. "I'm sorry, Leatrice."

I heard clicking, as if she were typing on her keyboard.

I looked at Tay, apologizing with my eyes. "Don't worry about it, man," he said. "You didn't know. She's okay with it now."

"I can hear you guys," she said. "It is estimated that hundreds of babies are sacrificed each year throughout our country, and even more in India. The reason we don't have more specifics, this Web site says, is because many of the women who plan to offer their babies up for sacrifice hide the fact that they are pregnant in the first place. The information we do have comes from people who have escaped the cult and informed authorities. And the word *escaped* is the word used in the article I'm reading."

My throat felt dry. Where was Stacey? She was now mixed up in all of this. Was her life actually in danger? If they were going to risk putting a child into a fire, would they give a second thought to killing Stacey?

Chapter Forty

Sitting with Tay in Java Brew, with Leatrice participating in the conversation via the speakerphone on my cell, we realized one thing for certain: there was going to be a wedding. Nancy, who was pregnant, was getting married. It wasn't entirely clear to me whom she would be marrying, or where the wrist-wrangling wedding would take place, but Tay, Leatrice, and I strongly suspected we had less than an hour to put the rest of the puzzle pieces into some kind of order.

"So there is definitely going to be a wedding, a handfasting," Leatrice said.

"Makes sense," I agreed.

I picked up the phone from the center of the table, and we headed back to my car, taking our coffees with us. "Nothing inside New Forest Church suggested that a wedding would happen there tonight," I said.

"That's because we're thinking like Christians," Tay said.

We got into the car. "And that's supposed to mean what?"

"When is the wedding?" he asked.

"Tonight," Leatrice said.

"Yeah, but when?" he asked.

"Midnight," I ventured.

"Under what?" he asked. I didn't understand the question.

"A waxing crescent moon," Leatrice said. I was still lost.

"It's an outdoor ceremony." Tay spelled it out for me. "The problem of finding out *where* is now even more difficult. At least we could have grabbed a phone book and hit all the, I don't know, Wiccan churches?"

"Oh yeah," I said. "That would have been real simple."

"Maybe they meet behind their church, out in the woods or something," Leatrice said.

And then it hit me. I started the engine. "I have an idea where the wedding will be!" I pulled out of the parking lot.

"Where?" they asked in unison.

"Not behind their church, behind my church. In the fields behind Faith Community," I said. "There was this guy out behind the church. He thought I was one of the people who had spray painted the church. He was going to stop me. When I convinced him I wasn't, he told me about the people meeting in the woods back behind the church. He didn't say witches or warlocks, he just kept saying *'them.'* I think he thought they were the ones responsible for the graffiti. Whatever it was, he was afraid of *them.*"

I turned the wheel and headed west on Latta.

"*Them,*" Tay said, using a deep tone of voice.

"But we don't know for sure that the people we're looking for are the same as *them,*" Leatrice said.

"We don't even know if this guy is sane," Tay added.

"True, but it feels right. Something about it—I know it's people from New Forest. And if I was a gambling person, I'd put money on the table that says they did the graffiti, too," I said.

"It's a quarter after eleven," Tay pointed out. "We have nothing else to go on. So at this point, your hunch might be as good as it's going to get."

Before we reached Faith, I could tell something was on Tay's mind. It was in the way he sat. His right knee was up, his elbow rested on it, and his teeth nibbled at the skin on his thumb around the nail. "What's up?" I asked.

"Just thinking," he said. It was more than just

thinking. We'd known each other too long. This was the tricky part, though. Not unlike me, he sometimes needed to be pushed into talking. It's a stereotype that men don't talk about their feelings—especially not with other men—but for us, anyway, it was mostly true.

"About?" I asked, keeping it simple.

"Remember when you became a Christian?" he asked. He moved his hand away from his mouth and lowered his leg. He turned to face me.

"Sure."

"What made you become a Christian?" he asked.

I chuckled. "What are you talking about? I realized that I was a sinner and that if I died right then and there I'd be going to hell. I didn't have a relationship with Jesus. Sure, I believed in Him. I never doubted there was a God. I just never took time to get to know Him."

"And you decided it was time to make Him first in your life? Not just an equal cut of the pie, but first over the whole pie?" Tay asked.

"Yeah, I mean, yeah. What's this about?"

"Optimism." I had no idea what he was talking about. Tay said, "Earlier we were talking about getting the women back. You said you were trying to be optimistic. You asked me why I was so confident, and I pointed toward heaven and said, 'Need I say more?'"

"I remember," I said, shrugging. I was not following his line of thought at all. "So?"

"It was in your eyes, man. You didn't believe me."

"What?"

"Where's your faith right now? That's all I'm asking," he said. "I'm not judging you, okay? I'm not. But there have been times when I've wondered if maybe you became a Christian out of guilt."

This time I didn't chuckle. I laughed. Nothing was funny. It wasn't that kind of laugh. I felt insulted. "Where is this coming from, Tay? I don't know what you're trying to get at. I've been going to church for years, usually more than once a week. I go to Bible studies. I read my Bible at home. I spend lots of time praying. I just can't see what point you're trying to make. Guilt? Guilt? Where would the guilt come from?"

He opened his mouth to speak.

I pointed at him. "Don't say it!"

"Nicholas, man."

"I said, 'Don't say it!'"

I pulled into Faith's parking lot, parked the car, and shut off the engine. I was fuming.

"Look, brother," Tay said. "Like I said, I'm not questioning who you are, and I'm sure not judging you. I just wonder if you know for sure where you stand. Have you surrendered? Have you asked God to empty you of you and to fill you with Him?"

I remained silent. My hands gripped the steering wheel tightly. I had heard what Tay said. I respected him too much to not listen. And maybe I was listening because I needed to hear what he was saying. Did something in my heart want me to listen?

"When I was saved," Tay said, "I knew my relationship had nothing to do with religion and rituals. It was a friendship, really. I realized I not only needed God, but wanted Him to be first in everything I did, first in every choice I made, like He was a physical person—my best friend—walking right beside me all of the time. Some people might let themselves be killed to save someone else, someone who is good and worth saving, but when Jesus came, He sacrificed Himself for all of us—while we were still sinners."

"You don't have to preach to me, Tay," I said.

"I don't mean to," he said. He looked straight ahead. "We're about to head into the woods, man. I have no idea what's waiting out there. A part of me is pretty scared. I'm shaking." He held up his hand. It trembled. "During everything we've done so far, every step we've taken, I've been in constant prayer with God, Tommy. I believe God has blessed what we've done—even breaking into New Forest, if that's possible. I've never stopped praying for Nancy and Stacey's safety, or for ours."

I lowered my head. "I've been trying to do this on my own," I admitted. There had been some prayers, but not many. It was easy to follow God when things were going well, going my way. "I need to turn this over to Him?"

Tay nodded. "We need to turn this over to Him," he said.

"It's about surrender. I know that. I knew it, but now I feel it," I said. "I want to pray."

"Together?"

"I think I need to do this alone right now."

"I've got some praying to do, too," Tay said. He raised both knees, rested his elbows on them, and closed his eyes, covering his face with his hands.

I lowered my head onto the steering wheel and prayed, *God, I don't know about before. All I know about is now. Please forgive me for all of the sins I've committed. I'm tired of trying to do everything on my own. I might think I can do everything in my own strength, but I can't, and I don't want to. I want You, God. I need You. I want You to be first in my life. I want to do the things You want me to do, the way You want them done, when You want them done. Keep Your hand on me. Don't let me go. And guide me, Lord. Lead me to where You need me. You are so holy, so perfect and just. With You walking with us, we will be safe. I know this. Please give Tay and me the strength and courage we will need to find and help Stacey and Nancy. I have no idea what we're about to walk in on, but I feel afraid. I wish I could open my eyes and this would all be over.*

I felt tears in my eyes. I left them there and kept my eyes closed for just a moment longer. I waited, kept silent. It felt peaceful, like I wasn't alone in my thoughts. God was with me. There was no doubt. I sensed Him. Only a few times in church had I ever felt His presence this strongly.

I surrender all, Lord. To You, I surrender all. Let Your will be done, Lord. I pray this in Jesus' name. Amen.

Tay and I got out of the car. "Thank you," I said.

"We got flashlights? I mean, other than those penlights."

"Had one. Batteries died. Haven't replaced them," I said.

"Okay. Dark woods. Witches and warlocks. No flashlight. Makes sense," Tay said.

We skirted around the side of the church and headed through the open field toward the woods. "You know where we're headed in there?"

"Not a clue," I said.

"Right."

CHAPTER FORTY-ONE

Over the years I'd seen a number of B-rate horror films. They all resembled what was taking place at that moment. Two guys head into the woods. No flashlights. No idea where they are going. Certain to get lost, they press on, pretending to be the predator instead of the prey.

Watching those movies, I used to call the protagonists foolish. The house is haunted? Foreclose. The dead are climbing out of their graves? Flee the cemetery. The vampire sleeps in the basement during the day? Move to Utah. The answer is simple. Don't. Go. Looking. To. Be. A. Hero. Run. Instead. Despite all common sense, Tay and I had become characters in a B-rate horror film.

Parting dangling branches and overgrown bushes, we walked deeper and deeper into the thicket. My mind raced, asking God for answers to the riddles we'd been presented with. Farrar had written something about the parents of the baby being "night" and "day." That made no sense. I tried to remember all that I'd read in the journal from the basement of New Forest. There had to be a connection. Something. I knew I'd read something about parents in the one entry but just couldn't recall it.

We breathed a little heavily as our feet cracked fallen branches underfoot. Every snap caused us to pause and listen. My heart beat so hard and fast that I thought it might break ribs. The beat was like a drum pounding in my ears. I was conscious of my breathing—in and out, in and out—quick, shallow breaths. How close was I to hyperventilating?

"Fire," Tay said. We stopped. We were here. Someone was out there. The next step was crucial. "Now what?"

"I'm thinking," I said. We had nothing to use to defend ourselves. We had God. "Let's get closer."

Slowly and as quietly as possible, we advanced. The small fire grew larger the closer we got. Crouching behind a fallen tree, we saw that it was a huge bonfire in the center of a small clearing. The flames crackled, sending embers floating up toward the dark sky. The moon was not visible.

The scene before us resembled images I'd seen on the Web. People clad in hooded robes held large, wooden walking sticks and stood around the fire. They chanted, some in deep, low voices, others in high-pitched voices. Men and women were gathered. Call me close-minded, but the whole thing reeked of evil. Nothing about this could be right. It was almost midnight. They were hidden in the forest. They wanted the gathering to be kept secret from others. If they believed that what they were doing was good and right, they wouldn't be holding a ceremony in utter darkness, tucked away and out of sight from the rest of the community. I couldn't understand the words being chanted. I tried. I couldn't look away, either. I felt compelled to watch. Morbid fascination. Macabre curiosity.

One person in a dark maroon hooded robe stood outside the circle. He wore a plate-sized pentagram charm on a necklace. He did not have a walking stick. He held his arms out with palms up and head lowered. I could not see his face. This had to be the leader. I wondered if the man was Alex.

Tay tapped my arm and pointed.

On the other side of the flames I saw Stacey and her sister. They stood back-to-back, secured to a tree by rope wrapped around their bodies, binding their hands. Both women were blindfolded. My stomach dropped, then rose. I thought I might get sick. "What do we do?" I asked. I was out of ideas. I counted the people encircling the bonfire. One, two, three…. "There are eleven, including the leader."

"Okay," Tay said. "Let's do this."

Right. I still didn't know what we were going

to do. I didn't know what God expected from me. I wanted Him to speak to me, to say something like, *Tommy, run out there and point at all of them, condemn them for their sin, and they will scatter, falling to their knees in immediate repentance, begging forgiveness.*

Maybe my thinking that thought was God's way of speaking to me? Or was it just *me* thinking that God was speaking to me? I felt confused. "We should run out there," I whispered.

"I agree with you, but not yet," Tay said. "Look."

My gaze followed to where he pointed. Two figures were coming out of the woods. They stopped in front of the dancing flame, just a few feet from the person who wore the giant pentagram charm. These two were dressed in regular street clothes—jeans and coats. One of them was Alex Farrar.

The man with the pentagram turned his hands over and held them up, silencing the chant. Those around the bonfire turned their attention to the leader and to Alex and his friend. I could hear Nancy and Stacey now. They were crying, sobbing. My heart ached for them. They had to be terrified. Unable to see, they had no idea what was going on. They had to be wondering what would happen next. They had no idea that, for whatever reason, the ceremony had been interrupted.

Thomas Phillips

"Dad, you can't go through with this," Alex said. "It's not right."

Alex shook as he confronted his father. This couldn't be easy. I never had a father, but I knew people who did. Alex's father was more than just some man. He was a cult leader. What Alex did took courage. Two questions came immediately to mind. *Why was Alex stopping his father?* And, *What was Alex stopping his father from doing?*

Gerald Farrar removed his hood. He smiled. He looked around at those gathered before locking his eyes on Alex. "Now is not the time. The handfasting ceremony has already begun." He raised his hood over his head and spread out his arms, palms up.

The chanting resumed.

Alex would not be ignored. He charged the tree where Nancy and Stacey were fastened and began working the knots on the ropes. With his back to his father, he was not able to see the command given. Robed figures left the ring around the fire and went for Alex.

The man with Alex let out a battle cry and charged those about to attack Alex.

I looked at Tay. He was already standing up. He and I jumped the fallen tree and charged out of the woods into the thick of things. Our appearance startled everyone but stopped nothing. Two men had Alex by the arms and had pulled him away from the bound women. Alex's friend was on the ground with two men kneeling on his back, trying to grab his flailing limbs.

The rest of the robed figures turned on Tay and me.

We took a fighting stance, standing back-to-back. They encircled us. We moved in unison, keeping an eye on all of them. The last fight I'd been in was more than four years ago. I didn't want to hit anyone. I didn't want to be hit. My adrenaline was pumping, though. I bounced on the balls of my feet, ready to spring, ready to attack. All I could think about was Stacey. I wanted to save her. I wanted to help her sister. I wanted to help Alex and his friend. I wanted to get Tay home to Leatrice. Right now, none of that looked possible. I was out of control. I prayed for wisdom. I prayed for courage. I prayed for help.

"Stop!" Gerald shouted. His arms were raised, commanding control of the situation. "Stop!"

The thugs who'd caught Alex's friend had him up on his feet. Like Alex, he was held by the arms.

"That's right, Dad. This has to stop," Alex shouted.

Gerald seemed intrigued by us. Tay and I still stood back-to-back, ready to fight. The people around us had not backed off.

"Which one of you is Tommy?" Gerald asked.

"I am," I said, refusing to let my fear show. Sweating in November could be perfectly normal, especially next to a raging bonfire.

"Thank you for calling off the police," he said.

"You were the one who called me?" I asked. He nodded. I thought it was Alex who'd called. "You need to let Stacey and her sister go," I said, hoping it sounded like an order, one he couldn't refuse to follow.

When he laughed, I knew I'd not made my point.

"You have no idea what's going on," he said.

"Oh, but I think I do," I said.

Gerald parted the people. They moved like zombies and came to stand behind Tay and me. They were like Wiccan church members and part-time security guards.

"Please tell," Gerald said.

I heard Stacey call quietly for me. She said my name over and over. She was still crying. She and Nancy were on the other side of the fire. I couldn't see her. I knew she was all right, and for now that would have to be good enough.

"You plan to marry Nancy," I said. "This is a handfasting ceremony—held under a waxing crescent moon." The pieces were there, jumbled in my head. I needed to work the puzzle out now. I was out of time.

Gerald laughed.

"You want her unborn child," I shouted, getting his attention. The night was silent. All I heard was the crackling of the fire, the beating of my heart, the sound of my breathing. Though I stared directly at Gerald, my peripheral vision seemed to explode inside my eyeballs. The red, orange, and blue flames blended with the people in green, red, and black robes. The trees towering over us seemed to sway and stretch and blend into one another. It felt like a dream. I prayed for focus. I prayed for protection from evil. "You want to deliver her baby and sacrifice it to your monstrosity of a god, Molech!"

Gerald's smile vanished.

"They know, Dad!" Alex shouted. He started laughing, the way a person does when a huge burden is lifted off their shoulders. "It's not a secret. They know."

Gerald did not seemed fazed by his son's outburst. He never took his eyes off me.

I pressed my luck. "Murdering an infant…."

"It will not be murder," Gerald said. "The fire will cleanse him, purify him. He is the chosen one, sent to fulfill the prophecy. As he grows and rises to great power, he will crush those who oppose him," he said, closing his fingers into a fist for an

316

illustration. "He is destined to be the leader of a unified world!"

"He's not the chosen one, Dad," Alex cried. "He's not the chosen one!"

Night and day. The parents. "What is night and day about you and Nancy?" I asked.

Gerald shook his head, confused. "What?"

"In the journal, in the office down in the basement of your church," I explained. "Did you write that?"

Gerald's eyes narrowed. His jaw shut; he ground his teeth, sending visible ripples through his cheeks. "I did not write that. The prophecy was written long, long ago. It will be fulfilled with the birth of Nancy's child."

"He's lying," Alex shouted. "He wrote the prophecy. He wrote it!"

"That's enough!" Gerald shouted.

"And you are the father? Does that make you night or day?" I asked.

Gerald walked closer to Tay and me. He put his hands behind his back, as if he'd laced them together for a casual stroll. "I am not the father," he said with a snarling smirk on his face. "The pastor of your church—the day—is the father. Nancy, a witch—the night—is the mother."

I felt as if I'd been punched in the stomach. I could not breathe. I felt light-headed. Things seemed to be spinning around in front of my eyes, or I was spinning. My pastor was the father. I couldn't believe it. I didn't want to believe it. This was crazy. Crazy.

"But don't you get it, Dad. The pastor isn't pure. He can't be the day!" Alex shouted. "You're misinterpreting your own prophecy!"

For the first time, Gerald took his eyes off me and focused on his son. "Who are you to question me about my interpretation of the book of prophecy?" Gerald's voice was gravelly, deep, and threatening.

The man was crazy.

"When the pastor found out she was pregnant, he wanted her to have an abortion," Alex declared. Like another punch to my gut, Alex's words almost made me stumble forward. I needed balance. What was the truth? "That is not day—that is not the father of good, by any means. And if anything, Nancy's not one of us—not anymore. She gave her life to Christ, like it or not. She turned her back on our faith."

"She came to us, with child!" Gerald shouted.

"She came to me, a friend," Alex said, "when she felt she had nowhere else to turn."

Gerald was quiet, contemplating. He turned his back on all of us and took ten paces toward the trees, away from the fire. His prophecy was wrong.

His son was right. Gerald couldn't deny all he'd just heard.

Another thought entered my mind, but I shut it immediately away.

"Let us go," I said. "There's no reason to keep us here."

Gerald turned to face me. "I can't let you go. There's no letting you go."

I looked at Tay. Gerald was responsible for kidnapping at the very least; he planned to murder an infant at the time of its birth. If he let us go, there was nothing to stop us from going to the police.

We needed to make a run for it but couldn't. Nancy and Stacey were still tied to the tree. "Get out of here," I whispered out of the side of my mouth to Tay.

"No way," he whispered back.

Alex and his friend struggled to free their arms.

Gerald raised his hood and then his arms. The chanting started up again. It sounded like one continuous, murmuring moan.

They circled around Tay and me.

Those big wooden walking sticks looked a lot like baseball bats. Wielding them like swords, the robed people closed in on us, step-by-step, and I saw no way out of this mess.

"Tay, I'm sorry," I said. "God, help us!"

The Prophecy

A shotgun blast stopped everyone in their tracks. Nancy and Stacey screamed.

I half expected to feel the searing heat of bullets ripping a hole through my gut. When I realized I hadn't been shot, I looked at Tay. He looked fine. I turned and saw a familiar face. It was the old man who lived in the house along Latta Road, on the west side of the church. He was dressed in blue jean overalls and a baseball cap. He had the shotgun leveled at all of us, sweeping the barrel to the left and right.

The sight this old man saw had to border on the bizarre. The bonfire burned, the wood crackled. Eleven warlocks wore robes with hoods, four of them physically restraining Alex and his friend, while the others encircled Tay and me, resembling an angry mob ready to beat us to death with walking sticks. And last, but not least, he saw two women blindfolded and tied to a tree.

"No one move," he ordered. "You that reporter?"

"Yes," I said. No sense explaining.

"Go untie the women," he said. I didn't wait for an okay from Gerald. I left the circle and ran to the women.

"It's okay," I said.

"Tommy?" Stacey said.

I removed the blindfolds. They both had their eyes open wide, as if straining to see everything after being deprived of seeing anything at all. I worked on untying them. "It's okay now. We're safe. We're out of here. Are you all right?"

"We're okay, we're okay," Stacey said. She smiled. She laughed. She cried. I wiped tears away from her eyes as the ropes fell away. She launched herself into my arms. I held her tight for a moment. I cupped the back of her head in my hand and tried to absorb her trembling, tried to take away her fear.

"We've got to move," I said. I stopped in front of Alex.

"We're fine. He won't hurt us," Alex said.

"Alex," Nancy said. "Come with me."

He shook his head. "Run," he told her. "Get out of here. It's over."

It was far from over if I had anything to say about it, but now wasn't the time for bickering. Tay joined us and we ran to stand behind our savior—a crazy old man with a shotgun.

CHAPTER FORTY-TWO

After calling the police, I called Pastor Ross and demanded that he meet us at the church right away. The clouds in the sky were gone. The waxing crescent moon was out. There would be no hand-fasting ceremony tonight. Nancy and Stacey sat in my car; it was running, the heat cranked up high.

The old man stood with his gun cradled in the crook of his arm, barrels pointed at the ground. Tay and I kept our distance, though we were thankful for his impeccable timing.

Surprisingly, Pastor Ross was the first to arrive. He pulled up next to my car, got out, and looked at everyone quickly before settling his stare on the man with the gun. "Mr. Farmer?" he said. "What's going on?"

"Me first," I said. "I trusted you. I believed in you. You led me to Christ, man. You." I was crying, but couldn't help it. "You betrayed my trust, and the trust of everyone at Faith."

"Tommy, please, I have no idea what you're

talking about!" He held his hands up in passive surrender.

I opened my car door, revealing Nancy to him.

Pastor Ross dropped to his knees. Nancy lunged out of the car into his arms. *Cute.*

"How could you?" I asked. "How could you ask her to get an abortion?"

Pastor Ross let go of Nancy, turned, and looked me dead in the eye. "What are you talking about? I would never do a thing like that. Never."

"It wasn't him," Nancy said.

And then I knew. "It was Alan Reddinger?"

She nodded. "He was an up-and-coming preacher, he told me. He was going to break off from Faith soon, start a new church. If anyone found out we were together—before being married—and that I was pregnant…."

She didn't need to continue. The rest was obvious. Reddinger had wanted her to have an abortion to mask their sin, hiding it from everyone else.

"I couldn't do it," she said. "I wouldn't kill the baby. I want the baby."

"Is that why you left?" Pastor Ross said.

"I didn't want to ruin Alan's career," she said, lowering her head as if this were somehow all her fault. "I didn't want to run, I was just so ashamed. I'd made such a terrible mistake. I don't want to run. I am so sorry for everything. I'm so sorry."

The mo|Ech Prophecy

Pastor Ross looked at me. I nodded my apology. "I jumped the gun," I said. "I'm sorry, too."

He stood up, helping Nancy to her feet. "Though you could have come to me," he said, "I should have known to come to you. I knew something was bothering you."

She cried, wrapping her arms around him. "I was so scared."

The sound of sirens grew, closing the distance.

I shook hands with Mr. Farmer. "You saved us," I said. "Thank you."

A line of police cars came down Latta Road, sirens screaming, lights flashing. There were two fire trucks and an ambulance. They filed into the church parking lot. Some parked up by the main building, some parked near where Pastor Ross and I were parked.

Police officers jumped out of cars. Several must have noticed Mr. Farmer. They had weapons drawn.

"Put the down the weapon," someone ordered.

Mr. Farmer squatted, set down his weapon, stood up straight, and raised his arms in surrender. Tay raised his hands as well.

"I'm the one who called 9-1-1," I said. "Tommy Cucinelle."

The police grabbed Mr. Farmer and forced him toward one of the squad cars.

"He saved us," I said. "He's not the problem!"

It took another twenty minutes before there was anything even resembling a calm. Tay and I were split up. We each gave a statement, offering a rendition of what took place. I'm sure the police wanted to make sure our stories matched. Separating us ensured untainted testimony.

Pastor Ross leaned against his car. He was mostly out of the loop. Police talked with him at first. Once they realized he didn't know much, they left him alone. When I was done giving my statement, I walked over. My hands were stuffed into my pockets as I leaned up against the car beside him.

"Hey," I said.

"Hey," he said.

"I'm sorry about freaking out on you earlier," I said.

He laughed. "You did freak out, but the evidence was pointing right at me. If I were in your place, I might have thought the same thing. There's no need to apologize, absolutely none," he assured me. "I'm just kind of troubled, I guess."

"Pastor Reddinger?" I said.

He shook his head. "Yeah. He had me fooled. He was really doing well, writing really powerful sermons, and he had stage presence. You've been to midweek?"

The molEch Prophecy

"I've enjoyed his preaching," I admitted.

"Most everyone did. I told him in a couple years he'd be the senior pastor of his own church. I told him the Holy Spirit was in him, working through him. I told him he knew how to fire up a congregation, that he'd end up with a church twice the size of Faith if he kept at it," Pastor Ross said. "I think I put too much pressure on him."

"This is hardly your fault," I said. It felt awkward counseling a pastor. "Reddinger knew right from wrong. So did Nancy, I guess. But he understood the seriousness of his actions; that was why he wanted to hide them."

"Yeah, yeah, I guess you're right." Pastor Ross looked up into the sky. "He and I are going to have to have a long talk. I'm not sure if he's going to be able to stay at Faith. I think we're going to have to discuss his path forward."

I nodded sympathetically. I couldn't imagine being in his shoes, and was thankful I didn't have to be. I was about to walk away when he touched my arm. I stopped and turned to face him.

"I'm sorry I dragged you into all of this," he said. "I was wrong in doing so."

I shook my head. "I wasn't really comfortable with any of it," I admitted. "But I know you needed help. In a way, I'm glad you turned to me. I learned a lot about myself."

"I felt a little helpless. I knew I'd failed Nancy somehow. I just needed to make sure she was all right," he said. "And maybe I needed to know so desperately not so much for Nancy's sake, but to make myself feel better. Can you forgive me?"

"Forgive you? Nothing to forgive," I said.

He hugged me tight. I hugged him back. Forgiving Pastor Ross wasn't difficult. Everything he said made sense. If I'd been in his place, who knows, I might have done the same thing. I just wasn't sure if Faith was going to continue to be my church home. I'd see.

Behind the church, brilliant police spotlights sat in the grass, aimed into the woods, chasing the shadows away. It looked like daytime. Police teams dressed in riot gear made a beeline into the woods. The bonfire might still be raging, but I felt confident that Gerald Farrar and his warlocks would have moved on by now. If Mr. Farmer's gunshot blasts didn't have neighbors calling the police, Farrar knew that as soon as I was far enough away from him I'd be calling the police. Either way, he had to know the police would be coming.

I felt nervous. I had to keep my hand on my stomach to steady the fluttering of butterfly wings.

The mo|Ech Prophecy

I hadn't eaten anything since lunch yesterday. I knew if I did I'd be in serious danger of spewing it back up right about now. I saw Leatrice and Kali and Stacey sitting side by side. Stacey came to church today to see me. It was a start. If we had any kind of a chance—a real chance—I'd need to know that she was serious about growing a relationship with Jesus.

I looked at Tay. He winked at me. I tried to wink back, but both eyes closed and opened. I couldn't remember how to wink. Oh no, what else had I forgotten?

I stood, trying not to see all the faces of the people staring back at me. The lights were hot, much hotter than I'd expected. That was another distraction—I was sweating.

Tay said, "One, two, one, two, three, four."

I started strumming my guitar. My thin guitar pick felt as cumbersome as if I were playing with a quarter between my fingertips. We played Chris Tomlin's "How Great Is Our God" in front of Tay's entire church.

When Tay had asked me to join his band this week, I was sure it had been a joke. He'd been serious. He didn't want me playing with his worship team every week, but he wanted me to give it a go, strumming along to a few of the songs that I played pretty well.

Thomas Phillips

I was the only guitarist on stage. I stood next to the keyboard player and to the side of Tay, who was on drums. The bass player was on the other side of the stage. Somehow my fingers remembered how to play the chords. I closed my eyes. I felt the music. The power of the song filled me. The hundreds in attendance joined Tay's voice. And we rocked, bringing the house down.

We went to Phoebe's Diner for breakfast after church. Dominic was there. He seated us.

"How have you been, Tommy?" he asked as we all were ushered into the booth.

"Unemployed," I said.

"I've been watching the news and reading in the papers about everything that happened."

"I didn't want to walk out of here that day."

He nodded. "I understand. I should have been more understanding then, but what can I say?"

"I'd love to have my job back," I said. No sense being prideful.

"Can you start now?" He laughed. "I'm just kidding. How about in the morning?"

I stood up and hugged him. "That'd be perfect."

After we ordered, I cringed. Alex Farrar walked in. He approached our table. "Can I sit?"

The ~~mol̶Ech~~ Prophecy

He took a chair from a table near our booth and sat on the end. "I'm sorry about everything that happened."

"Thank you," I said, on behalf of the group.

"My dad wrote that book of prophecy after a vision he had. He spent months writing it. And over time he came to believe that it wasn't written using his hand but divinely inspired. I believed him—he's my dad. But a part of me knew he was losing touch with reality, I just didn't know what to do about it," Alex explained. "I'm sorry."

He slid an envelope in front of me. "It's a check," he said. "It's to cover the cost of having the spray paint removed from your church. I'm ashamed that I behaved that way. Tell your pastor I'm willing to turn myself in to the police if he thinks that's necessary. I was just angry. As Christians you profess love and peace and forgiveness, and then Nancy's told to get an abortion by a pastor who's responsible for her pregnancy in the first place. I lost control. It was all so hypocritical."

I understood how he felt. I had no idea what Pastor Ross would want to do. "I'll let him know what you said. And I'll see that he gets the check," I said. Alex stood and returned his chair. I stood and shook his hand. "Thank you."

He nodded and walked out.

I sat back down next to Stacey. She took my hand in hers.

"How's Nancy?" Tay asked.

"She's doing all right," Stacey said. "I know this will mean something to you guys; she prayed for forgiveness. She plans on going back to church."

We all smiled.

"I talked with Pastor Ross," I added. "Reddinger was upset about everything that happened, totally blamed himself. He decided to get off the fast track for getting his own church. He asked if he could keep working at Faith as an assistant pastor."

"What did Ross say?"

"He was going to think about it. I got the feeling that, in time, Reddinger will be preaching again," I said.

After work on Monday—and man, it felt good to be back to work, back to normal—I stopped at a floral shop and used some of the money Pastor Ross insisted I take to cover the cost of expenses from over the last week. If I hadn't missed so many days of work, I'd have flat-out rejected the money. Like I said earlier, God always provided. I bought a bundle of assorted flowers done up nicely in a bouquet and drove toward the city.

The mo‖Ech Prophecy

Once deciding that this was something I needed to do, I began to fool myself into having high expectations. Arriving at the apartment complex where my mother lived was more frightening than standing onstage with Tay's worship team. And as I parked in the lot, I hoped she wouldn't be home. I walked slowly to her building, up the stairs, and knocked softly. When she couldn't hear the knocking and I left, at least I could tell myself I'd tried.

When the door opened, my breath caught in my lungs. We stared at each other for a moment. It had been four years since the last time I saw her. She looked nothing like I remembered her looking. She was larger than life while I was growing up. Drunk, sure, but she always seemed strong—or maybe just loud. Now she looked small, timid, fragile. She looked old, heavy. Gray streaked her black hair. She wore no makeup.

"I was going to go to the cemetery, to see Nicholas," I said.

"You going to put flowers there?" she asked. She leaned on the doorjamb. I didn't think she was drunk, but she wasn't sober. I could smell whiskey.

I held the bouquet up. "Actually, these are for you."

She snorted and shook her head. She didn't take the offered flowers.

"I'm not mad at you anymore," I said. "I forgive you."

Her smile vanished. She stared at me, eyes narrowed. "You forgive *me*? You're not mad at *me*? Just who do you think you are?"

"I'm not here to fight," I said. "You weren't there for me. You weren't there for Nicholas. The booze has always been more important to you. You can deny it. We both know it's true. I'm just here to tell you that I forgive you. I want us to try to salvage our relationship. I think we still can."

She slammed the door in my face. I stood there for a moment. I set the flowers down on her welcome mat and walked back to my car. As I pulled out of my parking spot, I saw her in my rearview mirror. She wore a coat and stood on the sidewalk with her hands in her pockets. I backed up and got out of the car. I went around to the passenger side and opened the door. I had no idea what to say, and I was afraid that if I said the wrong thing, or too much, it would ruin everything. We drove in silence to the cemetery.

We parked. I grabbed two chairs that folded up and fit into drawstring bags from the trunk, and we walked in silence to Nicholas's grave. He had a small headstone that I had bought to mark his resting place. I set up the chairs and pulled out my Bible.

The ~~moJEch~~ Prophecy

Mom saw the Bible but said nothing. She sat on her feet, hugging her knees as I opened the Bible to the book of John and began to read. *"In the beginning the Word already existed. The Word was with God, and the Word was God. He existed in the beginning with God. God created everything through him...."*

ABOUT THE AUTHOR

Thomas Phillips grew up with a reading disability. He did everything possible not to read. It wasn't until he was in seventh grade that he finally read a book cover to cover. Now a voracious reader and prolific writer,  Phillips uses his accomplishments as a motivational backdrop for speaking at school assemblies.

Born and raised in Rochester, New York, Phillips has worked as a freelance journalist and currently works full time as an employment law paralegal. Since 1995, he has written more than sixty short stories, articles, and mystery novels. He writes regular book reviews for a variety of e-zines, teaches writing classes, and has led a Bible study for the homeless with the Open Door Mission. He has been active in his church since 1997.

When he isn't writing, Phillips plays his guitar, coaches his children's Little League team, and plots his next story. *The Molech Prophecy* is his first published Christian novel.

Phillips encourages e-mail from his readers. He can be reached at thomas.phillips3@yahoo.com, or on the Web at:

> myspace.com/authorthomasphillips
> shoutlife.com/thomasphillips